Only the Lonely

Joanne Nicholson

I dedicate this book to Scott, for his love and support.

CHAPTER 1

Decorating the function room with pale aqua and white helium balloons and streamers had been a fun way for Tiffany and her best friend, Gabrielle, to spend the morning. Tiffany looked out the pane glass windows at the panoramic water view below. She knew the scenery would be wasted tonight, becoming a vast blanket of darkness as the vibrant lights of the party would draw the attention away from the surging surf below, focusing the attention of the guests on her.

Nervous excitement bubbled in her stomach. At last, she was eighteen and keen to party hard. It would be the first time she could drink in front of her parents and the first time she could legally go dancing in a club. Being younger than most of her friends, Tiffany had felt like today would never come.

The girls retreated to Tiffany's home to get ready. Gabrielle had practiced her makeup skills by watching YouTube tutorials for the last few years, so she was in charge of hair and makeup. As music boomed in the bathroom, the girls giggled, danced and sang as they prepared for the exciting night ahead. Gabrielle styled Tiffany's long blonde hair into loose cascading curls and applied layers of makeup, sculpting Tiffany's face with powdered contour to give her a sophisticated yet sultry look. Tiffany had never seen her eyes look such a bright shade of blue as they did now, framed with thick black, fake eyelashes and glimmering bronze eye shadow. With little time left to prepare herself, Gabrielle slicked her dark hair back into a tight bun and masterfully applied her own makeup to give her a fresh, dewy look.

After the obligatory selfies, the girls corralled Tiffany's parents into the car to head to the party.

The shrill noise of a knife clinking against a wine glass quietened the crowd and everyone gathered around for the evening's speeches.

'Can everybody hear me?' Tiffany's dad, Dave, asked, projecting his voice to reach the back of the crowd. Murmurs and nods confirmed he could begin talking. He wrapped one arm around Tiffany's shoulders and the other around his wife, Sandra, hugging them each close by his side. Tiffany smiled tightly. She loved her parents dearly but was a bit embarrassed by their public display of affection towards her.

'Tonight marks a very special milestone in our

lives. Our baby girl, Tiffany, is finally eighteen and we have watched her blossom into an amazing young woman. It took a lot for Sandy and I to have Tiff, but we managed to create a smart, kind, caring, thoughtful and beautiful daughter. Thankfully, she takes after her mother in the looks department,' Dave joked.

A wolf whistle pierced the air and a lone male voice from the back of the room yelled out 'MILF'. The room erupted into laughter; while Tiffany watched colour creep its way up her mum's cheeks.

'Calm down, boys, she's taken,' Dave laughed as he leaned over and planted a kiss on Sandra's forehead.

'Anyway, back to the speech. Once Tiff was born, we just knew we had been given the most perfect little human being and so there seemed no need to have another child as we all know that you can't improve on perfection. We have spent our life documenting so many of Tiff's firsts: her first steps; losing her first tooth; her first day at school; her first job; her first car and, now, her first day as an adult. I can't tell you just how proud we are of our amazing daughter. We love you so much, Tiff.

'Looking around the room tonight, it is lovely to see so many of Tiff's friends here to celebrate this milestone. You are a great group of young adults who I've seen really look out for one another. It's such an exciting time in all your lives. You are all at the start of choosing your life's paths. Just take time to enjoy every moment, as these are the best years of your life. A time when you have barely any commitments and are free to explore and just enjoy living. You've all recently finished school and can now focus your energy on pursuits that appeal to you. I know Tiff is looking forward to never having to do quadratic equations ever again.' Laughter rippled through the room.

'Next year, she will start her double degree in communications and law at university and we just know that whatever she ends up doing with her degree, she will be a success in life. Please raise your glasses and toast our gorgeous daughter, Tiffany.'

The crowd lifted their glasses in unison. 'To Tiffany.'

'Now, I know that you guys are planning on partying hard and going out to nightclubs after the party. Can I just ask that you take it easy and don't overdo it? Please, none of you consider driving if you've had a drink and if Tiff is a bit worse for wear, can you ignore the silver heart pendant hanging around her neck that says to return Tiffany & Co. in New York. Just bring her home instead.' Dave laughed as Tiffany rolled her eyes.

'My dad is the king of Dad jokes.' Tiffany laughed and pecked her dad on the cheek.

'I'm not going to talk for too long, as that dance

floor has my name on it. I just wanted to say firstly that I love you, Mum and Dad. You're my best friends, parents and mentors. Obviously, I wouldn't be here without you. I want to thank my BFF, Gabby, for helping set up the party today and for being like the sister I never had. Finally, I want to thank you all for coming here tonight to celebrate. I can't wait to go clubbing with you all later, it's going to be LIT,' Tiffany said to cheers from the audience.

'We just need to do the cake,' Sandra interjected, 'and then you guys are free to party.'

Sandra lit the candles on the top of the cake that had been styled to look like a pale blue Tiffany's box, complete with a white fondant bow on top.

The crowd sang the chorus of 'Happy Birthday' and Tiffany blew out the candles.

Dave and Sandra wrapped Tiffany in a double hug and each of them kissed her cheek simultaneously. The 'Tiffany Sandwich' was what they had called their group hug since she was a toddler. Tiffany cringed as she tried to extricate herself from her parents' embrace. She didn't want to hurt them, but as an adult, she didn't really want her friends seeing her squished between her parents.

'We love you, gorgeous girl,' Sandra said quietly to Tiffany, her voice full of emotion.

'We're both so proud of you, Tiff,' Dave added.

'I love you both too,' Tiffany responded, giving

each of her parents a kiss on the cheek. 'Now, I have to go dance.'

Sandra and Dave watched Tiffany saunter off towards the dance floor, already bouncing to the beat of the pulsing music.

Dave wrapped his arm around Sandra's shoulders. 'We've done good, Sandy,' he said, kissing Sandra on the lips.

Sandra smiled widely. 'We're so lucky to have such an amazing daughter. I love you, Dave. To think of all the trials and tribulations it took to get Tiff. I was sure for a few years there that we would never have any kids. I couldn't be happier with the way our life has turned out.'

'I agree. I just can't believe how time has flown. It's hard to believe our baby is now an adult,' Dave said, staring at his beautiful daughter dancing happily on the dance floor.

'It makes you feel old, doesn't it?' Sandra said wistfully as she wrapped her arm around Dave's waist.

'I can't think of anything more that I would want to do than grow old with you, Sandy,' Dave said. 'Now, can I get you a glass of champagne to celebrate successfully raising an adult?'

'That sounds like a great idea,' Sandra answered, her smile faintly crinkling the laugh lines around her eyes.

The party continued for the next two hours, with the volume of the music slowly ramping up to the point that people needed to shout to be heard. As the night was beginning to draw to a close, Tiffany came up alongside Sandra and wrapped her arms around her mum, 'I wuv you, Mum. Thanks for this epic birthday party.'

Sandra laughed. She'd never seen Tiffany drink before and thought it was cute that earlier in the night she had been embarrassed to hug her parents, but now that she was intoxicated, she wanted to hug her mum.

'I love you too, Tiff,' Sandra replied. 'Maybe you should slow down on your drinking and have some water.'

'Muumm, it's my birthday, I'm gonna party like it's my birthday,' she sang.

Sandra giggled at Tiffany's goofy antics. 'You dancing and singing tonight reminds me of when you were little and you used to put on cute concerts for Dad and me. Do you remember them?'

'Yep. I shoulda been a pop star,' Tiffany said, twerking in front of her mum, before bursting into a fit of hysterics.

Sandra laughed at the absurdity of her daughter's actions. 'Nice moves, Tiff! Please promise me that you will stop drinking if you start to feel dizzy. We don't want you passing out on your birthday.'

'I'll be okay,' Tiffany replied, nodding her head

in an exaggerated manner.

'Are you still staying at Gabrielle's place tonight?' Sandra asked, her responsible motherly instinct kicking in.

'Yep. I'll call you in the morning.' Tiffany kissed her mother's cheek before walking away.

'Ok. Have a fun time Darling,' Sandra called out to Tiffany's retreating back. Tiffany raised a thumb to signal she had heard her mum before she was enveloped into the throng of teenage friends, all ready to head off to a nightclub to prolong the party.

After the straggling guests finally filtered out of the room, Sandra's sister, Jody, and her husband, Alex, helped Dave and Sandra clear the room of its decorations. Each of them took turns couriering gifts from a present table to the boot of Dave's car.

With a final glance around the room to ensure they hadn't left anything behind, Sandra lifted up a box containing the remnants of the birthday cake. Exhausted but happy, Sandra thanked Jody and Alex for their help. It didn't seem that long ago Sandra had been helping out with Jody's sons' twenty-first birthdays. Jody hadn't suffered the same issues with fertility as Sandra and had been young when she started her family. Her sons were now grown adults living away from home.

'Thanks for a great night,' Jody said, hugging Sandra.

'I think Tiff will have a sore head in the morning,' Alex added.

'Yes, but you're only young once,' Dave said as he shook Alex's hand.

'We've all been there,' Alex responded laughing. 'Bye, Sandra,' Alex said before kissing Sandra's cheek.

'Thanks again for your help, guys. See you soon.' Sandra waved as they headed towards their car.

Leaving the nightclub, Gabrielle guided Tiffany towards the Uber. Gabrielle had been prepared for Tiffany to be really drunk – it was to be expected on your birthday. Gabrielle had made sure she hadn't drunk too heavily as it was her responsibility to get them both home safe.

Although Tiffany's hair had started the night styled into loose blonde waves that lay down her back, Gabrielle noted Tiffany's enthusiastic dance moves throughout the night had drenched her hair in sweat, leaving the back of her hair fuzzy and untamed. Tiffany's makeup was smudged under her eyes and any trace of lipstick had disappeared hours before. Although Tiffany wasn't looking as polished as she had to start the night, Gabrielle had never seen her looking so happy.

'That was an epic night,' Tiffany slurred, 'wasn't

it just the best night ever, Gabby?'

'Yes, it was,' Gabrielle agreed.

'Have you had a busy night?' Gabrielle asked the driver.

'It's been hectic,' the driver replied. 'There was a two car accident over on Pittwater Road. Apparently, three people were killed. A young guy has been arrested for drink driving. It's been a pain in the neck. The roads have been gridlocked for hours and it's been a nightmare to get around. I'm going to bypass that area. I think it will be another few hours until all lanes are opened again as they have cops out doing forensics to find out what happened.'

'Wow, that's sad,' Gabrielle replied.

'Let's not talk about sad stuff tonight. Tonight is a night of celebration. I'm finally eighteen, woohoo,' Tiffany hollered.

'Congratulations. Sounds like you've had a great time,' the driver replied.

'Yep, best night ever. I couldna done it without my best friend, Gabby. She's such a great person. You know I wuv you, Gab.' Tiffany wrapped her arm around Gabrielle's neck to pull her into a hug, which was more like an awkward headlock.

'I know, Tiff,' Gabrielle said, laughing at her friend's continual declarations of love.

'Don't lafffff, it's true. You're the best fwend anyone in the whole wide world could ask for,'

Tiffany continued.

'Thanks,' Gabrielle responded.

'I don't know what I'm gonna to do when you move away to uni. Life just won't be the same without my Gab-adaba-doo around.'

Gabrielle laughed. 'You're such a dag.'

'I'm getting tired now.' Tiffany yawned. 'It's really late, isn't it?'

'It's after 3am. I can't wait to get to bed. It's been a huge day,' Gabrielle replied.

Tiffany rested her head on Gabrielle's shoulder, 'hey, Gab, are you going to come to my place tomorrow to help me open my presents? It's going to be like Christmas but just for me. I wonder what people got me.'

'I can't wait to see what you got. You're so spoilt, I've never seen so many gifts,' Gabrielle said.

'I'm not spoilt,' Tiffany replied defensively.

'I didn't mean it like that, I was just saying lots of people spoiled you with heaps of gifts. Remember, anything you don't like, I get first dibs on,' Gabrielle said.

'Okay, but only cos you're my best fwend in the whole world. I'm so lucky to have you as my BFF. We will be best friends forever and ever. I love you,' Tiffany said.

The following morning, Tiffany cracked open

one eye, the bright sunshine coming through the window an assault to her senses. Her head throbbed and she hadn't even lifted it off the pillow yet. She had a dry, stale mouth and her stomach churned.

She closed her eyes and lay still, reflecting on the fun times of the night before. She was keen to look at the photos and videos taken at her birthday party before her phone battery had died. She crawled out of bed, rifled through her handbag and plugged the phone into a charger before returning to the warmth and comfort of the cocoon she had made from the bed on Gabby's floor.

As Tiffany lay still, trying to come to terms with her chronic hangover, she listened to her phone vibrating with constant alerts. She was sure 90% of them would be friends updating their Instagram stories, sending messages in Snapchat and tagging her in Facebook posts.

Gabby rolled over in her bed and looked at Tiffany. 'How are you feeling today, Birthday girl?'

'Argh, I don't think I've ever felt this sick. My head is throbbing. How can such a good night lead to such a horrible morning?' Tiffany replied.

'How about I get you some tea, toast and some painkillers? We have to leave soon to go to your place and check out your gifts,' Gabby said.

'Gab, you're the best. Hopefully, after I have some breakfast I will start to feel human again,' Tiffany said as she massaged her temples.

'There's nothing better than toast to soak up last night's alcohol. I'll be back in a second,' Gabby said, rising out of bed.

Tiffany lay still, breathing deeply to try to counteract the waves of nausea she was feeling. After a few minutes, Gabby returned with tea and toast.

Tiffany propped herself up in bed, trying to move slowly in an effort to not jolt the sharp pain in her head. She took a tentative bite of her toast then followed it with two paracetamols to ease her headache.

'Could you pass me my phone? It's been buzzing constantly,' Tiffany asked, trying to stomach another bite of toast.

'You're a popular girl,' Gabby said, passing Tiffany's phone to her.

Tiffany had a few missed calls from her mum and aunty. She knew they would be impatient for her return so they could see her presents. She listened to her voicemail. The first message was from her mum at 11.30pm last night, *Hi, Sweetheart, your phone must have died. I just wanted you to know that Dad and I are going for a walk in the morning. We will be back around 10am. We can come and pick you girls up from Gabby's place any time after that so you can open your presents. Bye, Sweetheart, love you.*

Tiffany's parents loved to walk. Her mum often spent weekends in her Lorna Jane activewear, her blonde hair pulled back into a ponytail that poked through her cap. Her dad, on the other hand, didn't look quite as stylish. He usually wore some old daggy tracksuit pants and a rugby jersey from his university days.

Tiffany played the next message from her Aunty Jody at 12.15am, *Hi, Tiffany, it's Aunty Jody, can you please call me as soon as you get this message.*

Tiffany wondered what could be so urgent that her aunty had left her a message in the middle of the night.

She moved on to the next message, also from Aunty Jody at 12.24am, *Tiffany, please call me, it's urgent.*

Tiffany's stomach tightened. The panicked sound of her aunty's voice made her feel uneasy.

She played the final message from 6.30am, *Tiff, where are you? Please call me ASAP.* Tiffany couldn't be sure but it sounded like her aunty had sobbed before hanging up.

Tiffany dialled her aunty. Even though she and Jody were close, it was out of character for Jody to call her in the middle of the night. It was answered on the first ring, 'Hello?' Jody said, her voice sounding strained.

'Hi, Aunty Jody, it's Tiffany. Is everything okay?'

'Where are you, Tiff?' Jody asked.

'I'm at Gabby's house. What's wrong?' Tiffany replied.

'What's her address? I'll come and pick you up,' Jody responded.

Tiffany recited Gabby's address. 'Aunty Jody, please tell me what's wrong. You're scaring me.'

'I'll be there soon and I will explain everything,' Jody replied before hanging up abruptly.

'What's going on?' Gabby asked.

Tiffany's stomach constricted. She had no idea what was going on, but her aunty was spooked. 'I'm going to be sick,' Tiffany announced before making a dash to the bathroom.

Gabby followed close behind and held Tiffany's hair back as she purged the previous night's cocktails.

Tiffany began to shake and cry.

'Tiff, what is it?' Gabby asked as she rubbed Tiffany's back.

'Something's wrong. Aunty Jody wouldn't tell me what it is but she is going to come and pick me up. I need to call Mum to see if she can tell me what the hell is going on.'

Tiffany raced back to the bedroom and called her mum's phone. It diverted to message bank. She tried her dad's phone but he didn't answer either. She knew they were going for a walk this morning, so they had probably just left their phones at home, but Tiffany had a sinking feeling that her aunty's panicked state and her parents being non-contactable were a bad omen. She dressed hurriedly and anxiously waited out the front of Gabby's house.

The moment Jody's car parked alongside the curb outside Gabby's house, Tiffany worriedly sprinted towards her aunty. The look on her aunty's face was enough to confirm there was something seriously wrong. Jody embraced Tiffany in a hug and began to cry.

'What's happened?' Tiffany asked, aware that she didn't really want to know the answer.

'I'm so sorry, Tiff.' Jody's lip trembled, 'I, um, don't know how to tell you. Oh my God.' Jody took a deep breath. 'Tiff, your Mum and Dad were in a car crash on their way home from the party last night. A twenty-year-old boy was driving under the influence of alcohol and he slammed into their car. They died instantly. He had a seventeen-year-old girl as a passenger who was also killed instantly.'

Tiffany's knees buckled and she wailed as she collapsed to the ground. The sound of her voice was foreign to her own ears.

Gabby sank to her knees next to Tiffany. 'Oh, Tiff, I'm so sorry.' Tears streamed down her face. 'That was the accident the Uber driver was talking about last night. I had hoped the young guy wasn't someone we knew, I never expected the people that died could have been your parents.'

'It can't be true. I just listened to a message from Mum on my phone this morning. This has to be a mistake,' Tiffany said.

Jody sobbed hard. 'I wish it was, Tiff. I went to the hospital last night to ID your parents. If it is any consolation, they didn't suffer. They probably didn't even know what hit them.'

Tiffany turned her head and vomited. The bright yellow bile puddled on the fresh green grass. It smelt as if it had just been distilled. She knew the smell of spirits would be etched in her mind forever as a trigger to remind her of this moment.

'Tiff, you need to remember how much they loved you and how proud they were of you. Last night they were both glowing with pride and the three of you were so happy. It's nice that your last memory of them is celebrating with you and all three of you declaring your love for one another,' Gabby said, hugging her best friend tightly.

'I want to see them,' Tiffany turned to Jody.

'I can take you, but you need to know that they look pretty bruised and battered by the accident,' Jody replied, grimacing.

'I have to say goodbye to them.' Tiffany collapsed to the ground once more, her arms and legs shook uncontrollably with tremors.

'Of course. I'll take you there whenever you are

ready,' Jody replied.

'How am I going to live without them? Where am I going to live?' Tiffany covered her face with her hands.

'Tiff, you can come and live with Alex and me. We will always be here for you. Anything you need, you can rely on us,' Jody said, hugging her niece.

Tiffany's heart physically ached as if it had been constricted and her stomach felt like she had been punched in the gut and winded. Her breathing raced and she felt light-headed. Her extremities were numb with pins and needles.

'Shhhh, Tiff. You need to take some deep breaths or you will hyperventilate,' Jody said, trying to calm her niece.

Tiffany shuddered. 'I want to die too. They can't leave me alone here. It's not fair.'

'You're not alone, Tiff, we are all here for you. Just think of all the people who were at your party last night who love and adore you. We are going to be your support network and will always have your back,' Gabby said between sobs.

Tiffany took some deep breaths. Once she had managed to calm down slightly, she turned to her aunty. 'Can we go to the hospital now? I want to see Mum and Dad one last time.'

Tiffany followed a white-coated man into a

sterile room in the morgue. Her parents had been so warm and full of life. This room was the antithesis of where they belonged.

The man yanked a drawer open and pulled back a flimsy blue cotton sheet. Tiffany's dad lay still on the slab, the colour drained from his face, his chest not rising and falling as it should. He had a laceration on his forehead that had been clumsily stapled back together. Blood coagulated around the wound, reminiscent of the makeup he had worn when he dressed up as Frankenstein for Halloween a few years earlier. Tiffany expected him to crack into a smile and tell her it was all a practical joke. She held his hand. It was stiff and cold.

Tiffany sobbed. 'You always protected me, but who was there to keep you safe? I can't believe you even lectured all my friends last night not to drink and drive. This is so unfair. You and Mum were my world, Dad. I'm going to miss you so much.' She half expected him to respond, wrap her in his arms and pull her into a 'Tiffany Sandwich' with her mum. The silence was deafening. She leaned over and kissed his cheek for a final time, 'I love you, Dad,' she whispered.

The scrape of another drawer opening behind her drew Tiffany's attention to her mum. Tiffany silently crossed the room. Her mum's once beautiful face was distorted; her eye socket was purple and the soft skin around her eyes bulged from the impact of the accident, erasing any hint of smile lines that were a part of her identity. Tiffany's anger flared. The stupid boy who had recklessly slammed into her parents had robbed them of any further joy and laughter. He had left her orphaned and alone.

Jody came alongside Tiffany and rubbed her back gently. 'Are you okay?' she asked sombrely.

Tiffany grunted. She would never be okay again. She wanted to scream at the injustice of it all and she abstractly pondered the fact that there was no way it would disturb anyone in this room full of refrigerated drawers.

Tiffany took a deep breath. She knew she had limited time to be with her mum and that it would be a waste to spend that time venting.

She leaned forward and smoothed her mum's hair back. It was still straight and smooth like it had been when she had left the hairdressers the day before. Her blonde hair was like a silk curtain framing her hideously distorted face. Tiffany arranged it to cover the worst of the damage. From a distance, she looked like a sleeping princess still swathed in the designer dress she had worn to the party.

Tiffany held her mum's freezing hand to her own warm, wet cheek. 'Mum, you were the most incredibly supportive and loving Mum in the world. I would do anything to get you two back. I appreciate how lucky I was to have been born to you and Dad. There were times when I wished I had a sibling, but then I realised I would have had to share you with them. Some people think being an only child is sad and lonely, but I felt privileged to have you and Dad as my best friends. It might make me sound selfish but I am so glad I didn't have to share your love and devotion. I just hope that I turn out to be just like you. I know we look alike, but I hope that one day I can find the love of my life, like you did with Dad and be an amazing mum like you were to me. Losing you two makes me feel like I've had my heart ripped out. I promise you both that I will fight for justice to get the guy responsible for this locked away in prison.' Sobs racked through Tiffany's body like a tidal wave. 'I will always love you, Mum,' she said, kissing the back of her mother's cold and lifeless hand before laying it across her chest.

Tiffany turned around to find her Aunty sobbing silently behind her. Without words needing to be spoken, they hugged, providing solace to one another.

CHAPTER 2

Tiffany was drained and emotionally spent after the visit to the hospital. Although she had been invited to stay at her aunty's house, she wanted to spend the night alone in her family home.

After locking the front door behind her, she stared at the living room through a new set of eyes. The room that she had barely noticed before was now steeped in history. She had sat upon her father's lap as a little girl in his worn leather recliner chair and sat side by side with her mother on the shabby chic floral lounge as her mum had tried to show her how to crochet.

On the shelf was a large framed photo of the family standing on a beach in Fiji, arms interlinked, faces bathed in sunshine and sand in between their toes. The smiles radiating from the photo were of a time and place that would now forever be out of reach. Tiffany grabbed the photo and hugged it to her chest as she slid down the wall and collapsed on the cold, hard cream porcelain tiles.

She sobbed, struggling to catch her breath. Tears

streamed down her face and her head ached. As a child, whenever Tiffany had been unwell, she had set up camp in her parents' bed where her mum would lovingly tend to whatever ailed her. Tiffany wearily got up and climbed the stairs to her parent's bedroom. She walked softly, her feet sinking into the thick plush beige carpet. Her mum's dressing gown was strewn across the winged-back chair that sat in the corner of the room. Nothing had changed since the moment her parents had left for the party. Tiffany pulled back the doona on the bed and climbed in, hoping the comfort of the bed would envelop her and make everything better as it had when she was a child.

The pillow smelt of her mum, a mixture of her perfume and shampoo, an aroma that was the personification of a warm hug on a cold night, a loving word of encouragement and a shoulder to lean on. Smelling her mum brought about a feeling of serenity while simultaneously twisting the knife in her heart.

Tiffany reached under her father's pillow and grabbed his pyjama top and held it up to her face. She took a deep breath, inhaling the familiar musky essence of his deodorant and aftershave.

The day had taken a toll on Tiffany and with sore, hot, puffy red eyes, she gave in to exhaustion. With her eyes closed, she could pretend, if only for a short while, that she was lying in bed with her parents, still surrounded by their love.

Tiffany awoke a few hours later and it took a few minutes for her to get her bearings in the darkened room. For that short amount of time, she was oblivious to her grief. When reality returned to the forefront of her mind, she was overcome with a tsunami of sorrow.

Minutes turned into hours. The images of her parent's battered bodies were burned into the back of her eyelids. The injustice of their untimely death formed a knot in her stomach. She laid each of her parent's pillows beside her and pretended she was encapsulated in a 'Tiffany Sandwich'. The realisation that her parents would never hug her again set off a fresh wave of tears.

As the birds outside began to stir and the first rays of sunshine filtered through the blinds, Tiffany gave up on sleep and, instead, decided to walk around the house, making a mental snapshot of all the memories she could invoke. She imagined her mum sitting in the winged-back chair in her room, her legs curled under her, sipping tea from her favourite mug adorned with embossed butterflies as she read her latest book. She recalled her dad lying back in his comfortable leather recliner in front of the TV, watching his favourite football team playing on a Sunday afternoon, yelling at the ref anytime penalties went against his team. As she walked into the kitchen, her heart ached that they would never again sit together around the white-washed wooden table talking about the events of the day. Tiffany hated the fact that the last time her parents had tried to give her a 'Tiffany Sandwich', the night of her party, she had squirmed out of it, worried about how childish she would look. She would give anything now to be wedged between her parents, safely cocooned in their love.

Sitting at the kitchen table, Tiffany lightly traced her fingertips across the marks in the wooden surface. Each scratch was a remnant of their family's everyday use. Something so banal now seemed significant, as there would no longer be an everyday event for them all ever again.

Tiffany lay her cheek on the cool, smooth tabletop. She was afraid she would start to forget what her parents looked like, smelled like, where they preferred to sit and all the times they had bonded over the years. She knew it was imperative for her to keep her parents' memory alive.

Tiffany's phone had died and she'd had no interest in charging it. The thought of seeing people's frivolous status updates or wading through people's pity for her made her stomach recoil. All she wanted to do was wind the clock back two days and keep time frozen in that moment.

The home phone rang. Its shrill sound jolted Tiffany out of her zombie-like state.

She answered the phone in a dull voice. 'Hello.'

'Tiff, it's Aunty Jody. How are you feeling, Darling?'

'Okay,' Tiffany replied.

'Honey, we have to start making plans for a funeral. Are you able to come to our place this morning to meet with a funeral director?' Jody asked.

Tiffany didn't know the first thing about planning a funeral, she'd only ever had to plan a party. She wasn't even sure that she was capable of making any decisions with her brain feeling so fuzzy, but she knew she didn't have a choice. She could almost hear her dad telling her to 'Suck it up, Princess.'

'Sure. What time?' Tiffany responded.

'He will be here at 11am. By the way, your parents made you the executor of the will but we thought Uncle Alex could help guide you since he is a solicitor. You are the sole beneficiary. Alex can explain the will to you. I know this is a lot to take on board, but there are official documents that will need to be lodged and he is happy to look after it all on your instructions,' Jody said solemnly.

'Okay,' Tiffany replied. Exhausted after being awake all night, she struggled to articulate herself.

'All right, well, we can talk about it all when you arrive. We will see you later. Don't forget to pack a bag so you can stay here,' Jody said before hanging up.

Tiffany grabbed a few items of clothing and threw them into an overnight bag. Looking around her room, she wondered when she would next be home and whether she would ever sleep in this room again. She struggled to come to terms with the fact that, suddenly, one day, everything that you took for granted could be ripped out from under you, leaving you lost and alone.

Tiffany sent a text to Gabby.

Can you come with me tonight to get a tattoo?

Hell yeah. What are you getting?

Something to remind me of mum and dad. I'm thinking a butterfly for mum and maybe a moon for my dad. Thoughts?

Why a moon for your dad?

Coz he used to read me that book about a rabbit loving its kid to the moon and back.

Cool. Have you checked out any designs?

Tiffany sent through images of some small

tattoos she had found online.

They look sooo good.

I hope I don't faint. Remember when we got immunized at school & I fainted in front of the whole school? I'm not great with needles tbh.

You should def have shots of vodka before we go for Dutch courage.

Good idea. Can you come to my aunty's place when you are free?

Sure. See you soon. xx

To Tiffany's surprise, the tattoo parlour was a brightly lit, sterile room. She had imagined it would be a small, dingy, dark room, run by bikies, but Tiffany was pleased that a small girl with bright red hair and a striking tattoo of a cherry blossom on her arm was going to ink her skin.

Tiffany handed over the designs she had printed out.

Sitting on the cold grey vinyl chair, Tiffany lay her arm out as if she was about to give blood. She winked at Gabby and took a deep breath to calm her nerves. She had never had a great desire to have a tattoo, but it seemed like the perfect way for her to carry a permanent memory of her parents.

The hum of the tattoo gun and the sharp pricks of the needle in her skin brought about a sense of relief. She was finally doing something that made her feel an emotion other than soul-destroying grief. Something significant to honour the importance of her parents.

Within ten minutes, the two small tattoos were etched into her skin: a small blue butterfly on her ankle and a silhouette of a crescent moon on her wrist. Once the body art was wrapped in sterile gauze, she and Gabby went to a nearby bar to have a drink.

Gabby raised her glass. 'Congratulations on being the first of us to get a tattoo. I would have put money on the fact that I would have been the first. They look awesome. Did it hurt?'

Tiffany looked at her bandaged wrist. 'Not really. It was actually sort of exhilarating. I think I might be hooked. I'm considering maybe getting my parents' dates of birth tattooed on my ribs. What do you think?'

'That would be sick. Next time, I might build up the courage to get a tatt as well.'

CHAPTER 3

Dressed in a simple black dress with kitten heels and with her blonde hair pulled back smoothly into a slick bun, Tiffany felt she had mastered the look of the stereotypical mourner. She had enlisted the help of Gabby to apply her makeup, which took forever. There didn't seem to be enough concealer to paint out the black circles that were in permanent residence under her eyes. Tiffany donned large black sunglasses to hide behind and tucked a white French lace handkerchief that she'd found in her mum's bedside drawer, inside her bra strap, ready for emergency use.

Flanked by her Aunty and Uncle on one side and Gabby on the other, Tiffany walked towards the front pew of the chapel. A sob escaped her as she took her first look at her parents' polished dark wooden coffins positioned side by side, one decorated in pink oriental lilies, her mother's favourite, the other was adorned by white lilies, a perfect complement. Her parents had always been in sync, in life and now in death. As devastating as it was to lose both her parents at the same time, there was a small amount of comfort in knowing that, in death, as in life, her parents were together.

Organ music played softly as people filed into the chapel. The stained-glass window bathed the mourners in a rainbow of bright colours, at complete odds with the sombre mood of the crowd. Tiffany gazed around the room, astounded by the number of people in attendance. There were not only her parents' family and friends, but a lot of her own friends were there to support her too.

Tiffany bowed her head. Her fingertip traced around the outline of the petite crescent moon tattoo on her wrist. She wondered whether her parents' spirits were watching over her and if they would understand that she loved them to the moon and back.

The minister walked to the front of the room. He was dressed in a white robe and wore a headset microphone, like a pop star about to perform a concert.

'We are gathered here today to honour and commemorate the lives of Sandra and David Parker – lives that were suddenly and tragically cut short. Sandra and David's lives have touched everyone here in one form or another and we all grieve their untimely deaths, but none more so than their daughter, Tiffany, who is supported here today by her Aunty Jody, Uncle Alexander and her cousins, Jack and Joshua. David's parents, Bob and Shirley, his sister, Helen, and her husband, Peter are also here to provide love and support to Tiffany in this time of grief.

'We may not understand why our Lord has chosen now to call them back into his loving arms but we can take comfort in knowing that as horrific as the accident was, neither Sandra nor David suffered when the time came.

'It is always sad to lose a loved one, but when lives are taken prematurely, it is natural to question the fairness of the situation and grieve deeply. None us can know God's plan, but in an effort to comfort you, I remind you of the passage in Mathew 5:4 *"Blessed are those who mourn for they will be comforted."*

'I know that you are all in a state of shock and you may need help in processing your thoughts and feelings. Of course, you can lean on one another to help get you through this difficult time, but I would also like to let you know that the church is also here to help. If you feel you need counselling or just a place for quiet reflection, you are always welcome within these walls.

'I would like to invite Sandra's brother-in-law, Alex, to give his eulogy.'

Alex straightened his tie and did up the top

button of his suit jacket before strolling to the
lectern.

'It is testament to Sandy and Dave that they
touched the lives of so many people given that the
chapel is overflowing today. Thank you all for
joining us to celebrate their lives. It was only just
over a week ago that we were all together,
celebrating Tiffany's eighteenth birthday. It was
such a lovely night and we will all have those fond
last memories to hold onto. I can tell you, I've never
seen prouder parents than Sandy and Dave as they
stood hugging Tiff while Dave gave his speech.'
Gabby squeezed Tiffany's hand.

'Of course, as you know, my wife, Jody, was
Sandy's sister. The two of them were thick as
thieves and she is going to miss her big sister
terribly. I met Sandy and Dave when I started dating
Jody more than thirty years ago. They were already
engaged and were inseparable. We aspired to have a
relationship as strong as theirs. I'll never forget the
expression on Dave's face on the day of their
wedding as he watched Sandy walk up the aisle
towards him. He was like the cat that got the
cream.' A small smile played at Tiffany's lips.

'They both enjoyed travelling and exercising.
Dave still played football with a team of mates
every winter. Their team, the 'Geriatric
Geronimo's', came runners up in last year's grand
final. It seems so wrong that a couple who were so

fit and healthy could die so young.

'Dave and Sandy both had fulfilling careers, Dave as a civil engineer and Sandy as a nurse. Over the years, I witnessed them both earn multiple promotions. The thing that a lot of people didn't know at the time, was that while they both seemed perfectly happy with each other and their professions, they were desperately trying for a baby. They both suffered so much heartache, firstly, by not being able to conceive naturally and then with several rounds of unsuccessful IVF. They had almost given up hope when their miracle baby, Tiffany, was born. She became the centre of their world and completed the last piece of the jigsaw puzzle of a perfect life.

'Being an only child, Tiffany had an extraordinarily close bond with both her parents. They were not just her mum and dad, but also her best friends. We know we can never replace them, but we want you all to know that Tiffany is like the daughter we never had and we will do everything in our power to help her transition throughout this period and grow into the amazing woman her parents knew she would become.' Alex's voice trembled and he stopped talking. Bowing his head, he took a deep breath as he pinched the bridge of his nose. The only sound that could be heard was the sniffing and sobbing of the audience. Once Alex was poised once more, he continued.

'Dave's sister, Helen, would now like to read a poem.'

Helen wore a black skirt suit, her dark hair worn in a smooth bob. She walked calmly towards the lectern and kissed Alex's cheek before adjusting the microphone.

'I'd like to read a poem I wrote called *"I am not gone"*.

'I may not be here, the way I used to be,
You cannot reach out and touch me physically;
But I will be everywhere you look,
The tallest tree, a babbling brook;
A petite butterfly in the sky,
The largest eagle flying up high;
I will be anything that brings my memory to you,
Because our soul connection will remain forever true.'

Alex took the microphone once more. 'Thank you, Helen, that was lovely. We will now have Tiffany's friend, Michaela, sing *"Arms of an Angel"* and if you wish, you may come to the front to lay a rose on the coffins and say your last respects.'

With a rose in each hand, Tiffany stood once the music began and walked towards the coffins. She was trying so hard to keep her composure. She simply kissed the top of each coffin before placing a rose down. She had said her last words to her parents when she had been in the morgue.

Slowly, the congregation rose one by one. Each person filed past the coffins, their moment to say their final farewells as they grieved the untimely death of their friends.

Tiffany stood to the side, accepting hugs and condolences from the never-ending stream of mourners.

Once Michaela finished singing, bland organ music began to play until the flow of people eased and Tiffany was able to take her seat again.

The minister walked to the front of the room once more. 'Today is a sorrowful day, but it warms my heart to see so much love in this room. Remember to be present every moment of your life, as you never know when this journey will end. Be kind and care for one another. The strength of another's love is powerful. Peace be with you.'

'And also with you,' the crowd chanted back quietly.

'Sandra and David's family would like to invite you all to join them for a wake at the Charleston Hotel for light refreshments.

'I would like to end today with the Lord's prayer. Please join with me.' The mourners recited the prayer by rote, a mumbled cacophony of voices.

Tiffany led the procession out of the chapel and was promptly swallowed up into a sea of dark-clothed mourners.

The wake was a simple affair, held at a local

restaurant. Tiffany looked around the room and assessed the guests. If she had been given the task of arranging a party for her parents, the guest list would have included everyone in this room. All her parents' friends were standing around chatting idly and the thought that her parents were missing out on their own party made Tiffany's heart ache.

Gabby sat next to Tiffany. 'How are you doing?' she asked, her face clearly showing her concern.

'Okay, I guess.' Tiffany looked at her friend and knew there was no point in lying. 'To be honest, I'm just feeling overwhelmed by everything. I just want to crawl into bed and stay there for the next year.'

'I wish there was something I could do to help take away your pain, Babe,' Gabby said, squeezing Tiffany's arm.

'I don't know how I'm ever going to be able to function again. I can't imagine my life without my parents. What am I going to do?' Tiffany gave up on her attempt to be stoic and let her tears fall freely.

'I'll tell you what you're going to do,' Gabby said, tears welling in her eyes, 'you're going to go to uni and make your parents proud by graduating with honours. You are going to be a strong, independent woman who is going to kick ass in life.'

Tiffany smiled as she wiped away her tears. She

knew she could always rely on Gabby to prop her up. 'Have I got mascara under my eyes?'

'Yep,' Gabby said, using a napkin to rub away the black smudges.

'Thanks, Gab,' Tiffany said.

'I can't let you go through the day looking like a panda,' Gabby joked.

'I meant thanks for everything. You've been my rock,' Tiffany replied.

'I will always be here for you,' Gabby said.

'Pinky promise?' Tiffany held out her little finger, as she had when they were children.

'Pinky promise!' Gabby replied, wrapping her little finger around Tiffany's before shaking them.

CHAPTER 4

Every aspect of life had become overwhelming for Tiffany. As she had inherited the whole of her parent's estate, she had to learn to manage it. Her Uncle Alex had helped her rent out the family home while she decided whether she would keep it or sell it. Every month, she handed him a pile of bills and he would pay them out of a trust fund account that had been established.

Tiffany's thoughts were focused on the looming committal hearing against the guy that had killed her parents. She wanted to see him locked away for life for killing three innocent people.

The morning of the first mention, Tiffany dressed in the same black dress she had worn to her parents' funeral. When looking at her reflection in the mirror that morning, she had noticed that the dress now hung loosely from her frame. Her appetite had been vanquished the moment she heard about her parent's death, leaving her looking drawn and emaciated.

Tiffany walked through the security checkpoint at the courthouse. Having her handbag scanned reminded Tiffany of being at the airport. On previous trips, her mum had always pulled over for the random explosives test. She and her dad had joked that she must look highly suspicious. Little memories like that flooded Tiffany's brain continually and she wondered whether the pain of such simple memories would ever ease.

Sitting in the wooden veneer courtroom, Tiffany breathed in the stale air. It was such an imposing environment and she was only the victim. She could only imagine how anxious a criminal would feel in this room. She wondered how many depraved people in the community floated in and out of this room on a daily basis. It was unsettling to be in a place where felons walked the halls.

With the support of her Aunty Jody, Uncle Alex and Aunty Helen, Tiffany sat silently in the gallery awaiting the hearing. She watched a couple, similar in age to her parents, sitting in the next row. The woman had a straight brown bob with a side fringe that she repeatedly brushed off her forehead. The man sat ramrod straight, his jiggling leg the only giveaway that he was nervously awaiting proceedings to begin. They both wore identical looks of stress and as the lady leaned towards the man to whisper to him, he wrapped his arm protectively around her shoulder. Tiffany wondered whether they were the parents of the driver and she spitefully hoped they would feel at least a fraction of the loss she had to live with if their son was sent to jail.

A solicitor entered the room with a young man dressed in an ill-fitting charcoal suit, his dark hair slicked down across his forehead. He looked wide-eyed and afraid. Had he been standing there for any other reason, Tiffany may have felt empathy for him, but every ounce of her compassion had been extinguished by the senseless loss of her parents. He turned and nodded at the couple in the next row, confirming Tiffany's suspicions they were his parents. His eyes briefly glanced over towards Tiffany but as soon as he registered eye contact with her, he bowed his head and looked down at the desk in front of him.

The Court Officer addressed the room. 'All rise. Manly Local Court is now in session. His Honour Chief Magistrate Petersen presiding.'

The magistrate walked into the silent room dressed in a robe and bowed in deference to the lawyers. They nodded in return, a ritual they completed subconsciously. Once the magistrate sat, the court followed his lead and took their seats.

'The first case to be heard today is the Crown vs Jefferson, H. Driving occasioning Death Section 52A(1) of the Crimes Act 1900. How do you plead, Mr Jefferson?'

Tiffany's breath caught. Her Uncle Alex had told her that if he pleaded guilty he would go straight to sentencing.

'Not guilty, Sir.'

A gasp escaped from Tiffany as she stared at the magistrate in shock. There was no disputing Harley Jefferson had killed not only Tiffany's parents, but also his girlfriend. His parents turned around to stare at Tiffany as she silently shook her head in disbelief.

The solicitor for the Crown rose. 'Your Honour, this man was culpable of the death of three people on the night of 27th of November 2015. He returned a blood alcohol level of 0.07.'

The defendant's solicitor rose. 'Your Honour, Mr Jefferson is a model citizen. He has a clean criminal record. He is young, still living under his parents' supervision, is a university student and is gainfully employed in a part-time job. He is remorseful for his actions. I respectfully request that these facts are taken into consideration to grant bail.'

'I find a prima facie case and commit this matter to trial in the Supreme Court, to be heard on the 2nd of August 2016. Mr Jefferson, given the information tended by your counsel, I do not believe you pose a flight risk. Bail will be granted for a sum of $1,000,' the magistrate said before neatly tidying up his pile of paperwork pertaining to the case. 'You are dismissed.'

Tiffany was in shock. The magistrate had simply transferred the case without hearing any evidence. She wanted Harley Jefferson, his parents and the magistrate to hear how his actions had ruined her life.

The people sitting in the gallery for that case filed out of the courtroom. Once in the hallway, Tiffany burst into tears. Her Aunty Jody wrapped her arms around her to comfort her. 'This is ridiculous,' Tiffany wept into her aunty's shoulder.

Alex rubbed her back. 'This is just standard for the system. There has to be time for each side to prepare a defence. We will all have to give statements to the Crown's solicitor to build the case and it will then be heard in front of a jury. I'm sorry I didn't warn you that today probably wouldn't result in a conviction.'

'It's just wrong that Harley Jefferson is free to go about living his life when three people have lost their opportunity to ever see their family and friends again. I hope that when it goes to the Supreme Court, they lock him up and throw away the key,' Tiffany said, anger making her voice quiver.

'Why don't you sit down for a moment and take a second to calm down? We just want to talk with the solicitor for the Crown to find out what he wants us to do next,' Alex said as he guided Tiffany to a bank of hard grey plastic bucket seats that were affixed to the ground, presumably to ensure they were not used as a projectile by someone in a rage.

Tiffany sat and rested her head in her hands. The whole day had been emotionally exhausting.

'Excuse me, Luv, do you mind if I sit here?' a lady's voice asked. Tiffany nodded numbly, being in no mood to converse with a stranger.

'I just wanted to offer my condolences to you. I know it must be difficult for you losing both your parents.'

Tiffany raised her head and looked at the stranger, a middle-aged woman with a brown bob and a strained look on her face. Tiffany's stomach recoiled when she realised the voice belonged to Harley Jefferson's mother.

'You have no idea how hard it is. Your son didn't die in the accident. He is still alive and well. Did you know I'm an only child? I'm now an orphan with no immediate family. With all due respect, I truly don't think you know how 'difficult' it is for me,' Tiffany responded venomously.

Mrs Jefferson's face bloomed bright red. 'I know that nothing I can say will take away the hurt. We are all devastated by the accident and the loss of three innocent lives. I just wanted to ask that you take into consideration that Harley is not much older than you. He has his whole life ahead of him. We can't bring back the lives of those who are gone, but does it serve any purpose to ruin my son's life for one stupid mistake? I just thought you might be able to ask for the case to be dropped or for him to get a good behaviour bond.'

Tiffany's blood boiled. 'You're deluded. How dare you suggest that he shouldn't be held accountable for killing three people,' Tiffany said, her voice rising. 'Your son is a murderer who deserves to rot in jail. My parents and his girlfriend all had their lives ahead of them too, until he killed them.'

Mrs Jefferson's hands shook nervously. 'I'm sorry to have upset you. That wasn't my intention. I'm just a mum who loves her son and I want to do anything in my power to protect him.'

'Here's a newsflash for you – I'm a daughter who loves her mum and I couldn't do anything to protect her or my dad from your son's reckless behaviour and now I'll never see them again. So just fucking leave me alone,' Tiffany yelled.

Security guards rushed towards Tiffany. 'Excuse me, Miss, please refrain from raising your voice. You are in a court of law. I ask that you please leave the premises or we will have to escort you.'

'I'm leaving,' Tiffany replied before she stormed off towards the exit, desperately in need of fresh air.

CHAPTER 5

Although she longed to just curl up in a ball and sleep away the day in an effort to block out her reality, Tiffany was forced to keep living life. Her Aunt and Uncle had convinced her that she must continue with her plan to start university and to live the life her parents had envisaged for her. Given the ongoing status of the court case against Harley Jefferson, Tiffany was motivated to start her law degree to learn about the legal system and help her parent's case progress smoothly and ensure justice was served.

Tiffany enrolled at Macallister University and decided to live on campus as she didn't want to be a burden on her aunt and uncle. She packed up her most prized possessions and moved them into a room in Dunkirk College. The room was like a reflection of her mood, a soulless, bare brick-walled space with no scope for aesthetics. It was functional with a single bed, wardrobe and a small desk. The brown nylon carpet smelt damp, which she hoped was due to the previous tenant's lack of hygiene and not an ongoing problem. The tiny ensuite attached had a small shower cubicle, a basin and toilet. She noted the grout between the beige tiles in the shower recess was white towards the ceiling but a dark grey colour down low where it had not been effectively cleaned for years. Tiffany knew her parents would have cringed at her new living quarters, having raised her in a spotlessly beautiful home, but she needed her independence and this little room would be the new start she needed to move forward.

After unpacking her clothes, Tiffany walked into the common room. A few students lazed about in mismatched lounges, sipping coffee and chatting.

'Hi, Newbie,' a bubbly dark-haired girl called out to Tiffany. 'Come and join us. We are just talking about tomorrow night's toga party.'

'Thanks. I'll just make a coffee first,' Tiffany responded. She wanted to settle in and make friends, but she found it hard to pack her grief into a recess of her mind and relax like everything was normal.

As Tiffany came towards the lounge, the enthusiastic girl jumped up, her dark brown curls bouncing as if they had a life of their own.

'Hi there. I'm Sarah, I'm doing primary teaching here. We all just moved in to the college yesterday. My mum was a blubbering mess. You'd think I had died, not just moved out of home,' she joked, the others nodded and laughed with her.

Tiffany smiled weakly. 'I'm Tiffany. I'm doing communications and law.'

'Ooh, we've got a smart one here,' Sarah said lightly. 'This is Mandy, she's from the country and is doing a BA, you know, bugger all.'

'Hey,' Mandy said, feigning offense, 'don't go dissing my Bachelor of Arts. I'm a creative genius and I'm planning to work out my major as I go along. You can't rush these things.'

'Hi, I'm Sunani,' an Indian girl said, thrusting her hand out to shake Tiffany's. 'I'm from Delhi and I'm completing my third year of chiropractics.'

'It's nice to meet you all,' Tiffany said before taking a sip of her coffee.

'Ok, so now we have all the awkward greetings out of the way, we need to plan what we are wearing to the toga party tomorrow night. Sunani, you should be able to turn a bed sheet into a toga. It's pretty much the same as a sari, right?' Sarah asked.

'I can wrap a sheet around you, but I can't guarantee it won't look like a sari,' Sunani said.

'That'll do,' Mandy said. 'I'll get some plastic ivy and make us wreaths to wear on our heads. How much do you think I will need to make four wreaths?'

'Oh, I'm not really up to going to a party. Don't count me in,' Tiffany added hastily.

'Don't be silly. It's 'O Week', you have to come so you can meet all your new uni friends,' Mandy responded.

'Come on, Tiffany, we need to get drunk, dance and meet boys. That's the real reason we live here, isn't it?' Sarah joked. 'How are we going to have private in-jokes and memories to reflect on together if you're not there?'

'I'm going to be living in the same place as you. I'm sure we will have plenty of time to bond over meals,' Tiffany replied.

'Boo hoo. You need to lighten up. You'd think we're planning a funeral, not a party,' Sarah said.

Tiffany's eyes welled with tears.

'What is wrong, Tiffany?' Sunani asked. 'You seem upset.'

Tiffany turned her face to the side and tried to swipe away her tears. 'Both my parents died late last year in a car accident. I'm finding it a bit hard to find any enthusiasm to party.'

Sarah rushed over and wrapped her arms around Tiffany's shoulders. 'I'm sorry. I always put my foot in my mouth. It must be tough losing your parents. How are you coping?'

'I have good days and bad days,' Tiffany replied. She didn't want to be the person that everyone pitied, but some days, small things set her off.

'Do you have any siblings, Tiffany?' Sunani asked.

'No. I'm an only child, so now I'm officially an orphan,' Tiffany responded.

'Darl, I miss my parents and even my brother and they are only a six-hour drive away. I can't imagine what it would be like to not have them around anymore,' Mandy said solemnly.

Tiffany took a deep breath. 'Anyway, now you know why I'm not feeling much like partying, but I don't want to be a downer. You girls need to keep planning so you are the hottest Roman Goddesses there ever were.'

'Tiffany, with due respect, I think your parents would be sad if you weren't having fun living your life. It's not disrespectful to them for you to have a little joy in your life. Heaven knows it sounds like you could do with some light-hearted fun after the past few months you've had,' Sunani said, reaching over to pat Tiffany's knee.

'Yeah, it's not like the olden days when you had to mourn for a year and wear all black,' Sarah added. 'Will you at least get dressed up with us and come and meet a few people? If you're not having fun, I will come home with you.'

Tiffany looked at all the girls. As much as she felt no inclination to party, she did want to form bonds with her dorm mates and after the past months of sadness, she felt maybe there was room for a little joy. 'Okay, I'll come for a little while,' Tiffany conceded.

Sarah squealed. 'Yay! We are going to be amazing goddesses. I just need a white bed sheet as my sheets have pink polka dots on them.'

'I've got some spare white sheets in storage. I'll go get them tomorrow,' Tiffany said, pleased to be able to add to the planning.

The following evening, the girls met in Sarah's room for their transition into Roman Goddesses. Mandy braided the girls' hair and wrapped the braids around their heads before placing her homemade plastic ivy garlands on top. Sunani wrapped bed sheets around them and tied them expertly. Tiffany had been designated to apply the girls' makeup, but Sunani politely declined, stating none of the colours in Tiffany's palette were suitable for her skin tone. 'You're so lucky to have such brown skin, Sunani. I had to spend hours last night fake tanning,' Sarah said, showing off her slightly orange tinged skin.

'Me too, I just use a darker shade,' Sunani joked, grinning widely. The girls laughed.

'It looks very natural,' Mandy replied sarcastically.

'I'm actually an Aussie, mate,' Sunani said in a bad attempt at an Australian accent.

The girls' laughter erupted into a raucous cacophony of sound. Tiffany could barely remember the last time she had laughed. It must have been the night of her eighteenth birthday party – the same night her whole world had imploded.

After a few vodka cruisers, the girls were in high spirits and ready to walk to the bar where the toga party was being held.

They entered the common room and were greeted by a circus of toga-wearing students. Tiffany felt glad she had relented and joined in the fun. If only for a brief window of time, she could feel something other than all-encompassing grief, it had to be a step in the right direction. She may not have a family, but standing dressed in a toga in the recreational room, she strangely felt that she belonged.

As Tiffany and her friends walked across campus, they revelled in the party atmosphere. A passing group of boys were using a wheelie bin as a chariot to transport another boy to the party. It seemed no one had a care in the world and Tiffany tried to embrace that feeling for as long as she could.

As they neared the bar, Tiffany could feel the base beat reverberating. The music was so loud, she knew it was probably impossible to talk once inside. She was sick of talking about her feelings, accepting people's condolences and dealing with the crushing thoughts of her recent loss. She longed for a night off to get drunk, dance and laugh with her new friends.

With drinks in hand, the girls hit the dance floor. Sweaty bodies, scantily dressed in an array of bed sheets writhed to the beat. Tiffany wondered if this was what life had been like in the days of the ancient Roman Empire.

After a few songs, the girls retreated outside to get some cool air.

'Okay, girls, which of these guys here would you want to rip their sheet off?' Sarah asked.

The girls gazed around at the half-naked men draped in bed sheets, standing and drinking, nodding their heads in time with the music.

'I wouldn't mind spending time with that Adonis,' Mandy said, pointing to a buff looking guy standing a few metres away.

'Adonis was a Greek God, not a Roman God,' Sunani clarified.

'I'm not racist. I'd take him regardless of what sort of God he is,' Mandy joked.

'How about that guy over there with the dark hair and broad shoulders, wearing the grey toga?' Sarah pointed across the crowd to a tall guy standing with his arms crossed across his chest, laughing with his mates.

Tiffany stared at the man, her blood rushed in her ears. 'No,' she said tersely.

'Is he an ex of yours?' Sarah asked.

'No. He is a murderer,' Tiffany replied. She was livid that Harley Jefferson was dressed in a toga at a party, like he didn't have a care in the world. He didn't have the right to be out having fun when he should rightly be locked away behind bars.

Having had a few drinks, Tiffany had the Dutch courage to confront him. She walked towards him. He smiled as she neared, her costume obviously altering her appearance so that he was oblivious to her identity.

'Hey,' he said as she reached him. She was seething that he had the arrogance to think she was interested in him.

'Do you know who I am?' she asked bluntly.

'No, I don't go to this uni. Should I know who you are? Are you Insta-famous or something?' he asked, smiling cheekily at his friends.

'I'm Tiffany Parker. You might remember me now. I'm the girl whose parents you killed last year when you were driving drunk.'

Hearing Tiffany's name wiped the smile from Harley's face. 'Oh shit. Yeah, listen, I'm really sorry about that. I wish I could change things,' he responded solemnly.

'Well, you can't. I can't believe you are dressed up in a fucking toga, partying with your mates. You don't deserve to be living a free life when you killed three people. I can't wait to see you locked up in jail.'

The surrounding guests had stopped their conversations and were listening intently to the argument. Tiffany's three friends stood in solidarity behind her.

'I understand how you feel, but don't you realise that I'll never forgive myself for what happened that night?' Harley replied forlornly.

'Well, that makes two of us, you douchebag,' Tiffany yelled, pushing her palm against his chest.

'I think it's time to go,' Sarah said, wrapping her arm around Tiffany's shoulder to guide her away from the commotion.

Once they were beyond the boundary of the bar, Tiffany collapsed to the ground. The alcohol, mixed with her fury and grief, had left her emotionally exhausted. Her friends consoled her and eventually managed to convince her it would be more comfortable for her rest on her bed than in the middle of the campus.

Tiffany woke with a start. Her body shook, her heart raced and an overwhelming feeling of helplessness engulfed her. She threw back the covers and sat up, trying to shake the vivid memory of the recurring dream that had plagued her for the last few months. In the nightmare, she was the skipper of a boat and her parents were swept overboard. Although she tried hard to manoeuvre the boat, the seas were so violent that she couldn't steer the boat to turn around to rescue them. She had to watch her parents disappear into the distance, being tossed about in the ferocious swell, without being able to do anything to save them.

Wiping the sweat from her brow, Tiffany walked to the bathroom to get a drink of water. She knew that the dream would play on a loop in her mind if she closed her eyes to try to sleep again. She decided that it would be better to scroll through Instagram and Facebook, hoping that vicariously watching what her virtual friends were up to would make her feel less alone and distract her from feeling useless.

Photos of the toga party dominated her university friends' timelines. Tiffany thought back to seeing Harley Jefferson, the smug son of a bitch, out partying. She wished she hadn't just pushed him, but instead, had punched him in the face. Heaven knows he deserved to have some sense knocked into him. Tiffany silently hoped that when he finally went to jail, he would become some big hairy criminal's punching bag. Instead of calming her down, being on social media was having the opposite effect, making her feel more agitated. Tiffany slammed the lid closed on her laptop and lay on her back, trying to calm her breathing.

CHAPTER 6

The following morning, Tiffany awoke with a piercing headache. Not only was she hungover from the alcohol consumed the night before, but she was still seething at the injustice that Harley Jefferson was out partying when he should be paying the price for ruining her life. As if that wasn't enough, she had humiliated herself in front of her new friends and the entire university co-hort. As much as she was trying to be strong, it didn't seem to be working. She didn't want to keep re-hashing her feelings with her Aunty Jody, as she knew her aunty was also grieving for her sister and didn't need the additional burden of having to put on a strong façade for her. As empathetic as her friends were, none of them could truly understand how she was feeling.

Tiffany reached into the side pocket of her handbag and retrieved a referral her doctor had given her to visit a psychiatrist for grief counselling. She didn't want to admit that she wasn't coping, but she couldn't repeat the previous evening's incident of having an emotional breakdown in the middle of the campus. After taking a deep breath, she dialled the number and arranged her first session.

Dr Grace Flanders was a middle-aged woman with a blonde pixie cut. She had a serene face with amber coloured eyes. Tiffany was instantly at ease with her as her calm demeanour reminded Tiffany of her mum.

'Please take a seat,' Dr Flanders said, motioning for Tiffany to sit in a worn leather armchair.

'Thanks,' Tiffany replied, offering a weak smile in response. She sat and sighed heavily.

'Tiffany, I wanted to start our session by offering my condolences for the loss of your parents. I'm glad you have come to seek help. In my experience, people who bottle up their problems don't cope well in the long run. Anything you say to me will be kept in complete confidence, unless I believe there is a significant risk of you harming yourself or others. I think we should start with you telling me about the night of the accident.'

'It was my eighteenth birthday party. We were having a great time. Dad gave an awesome speech littered with his standard dad jokes.' Tiffany smiled, reminiscing. 'I went out to a club with my friends and my parents packed up after the party. They were on their way home, stopped at traffic lights, when a car, driven by a twenty-year-old guy who was drink driving, slammed into their car. They were killed instantly, as was the driver's girlfriend who was seventeen. I stayed at my friend, Gabrielle's house that night. My phone had died and so no-one was able to contact me. The following morning, I returned a call to my Aunty Jody. She drove to Gabby's place and told me my parents had both been killed. I'm an only child, so I now don't have any immediate family. Aunty Jody and I went to the morgue so I could see my parents and say goodbye. My aunt and uncle have been a great support.'

'You're very brave to have told that story. I want to now dig deeper and ask you how you have been feeling.'

'I'm sad, angry, lonely. I have trouble sleeping because my brain keeps playing the images of my dead parents over and over. I'm frustrated that the court case is taking forever. I feel like it would bring some closure if the guy that killed my parents was finally in jail. I feel guilty because my parents wouldn't have been in the car at that moment if they hadn't been at my party. I also feel bad that no-one could contact me until the next day because my phone died.' Tiffany sobbed and tears streamed down her face. Her pent-up emotions made it hard to continue speaking.

Dr Flanders passed a box of tissues over to Tiffany. 'They are all very normal emotions. You may have heard of the five stages of grief. They are denial, anger, bargaining, depression and acceptance. When you heard of your parents' deaths, you would have been in shock. You had just been celebrating with them the night before. I'm glad you saw them in the morgue as it makes the whole scenario more real, meaning that you can't be in denial about their deaths. The second stage is anger and you are obviously angry with the young man responsible for the accident. You may even feel a little angry at the fact that your parents' deaths may have left you feeling abandoned. Although you have great support from your extended family, you have no parents or siblings to rely upon throughout the rest of your life. Bargaining is the next stage of grief where you wish you could do something in exchange for a different outcome. You feel guilty about having been out clubbing when they died, so for example, you may say something like, "If I could have my parents back, I'd never party again." Bargaining is a bit counterproductive because, as we know, there is nothing that will bring your parents back physically. They will, of course, always live on in your heart and through your memories. The next phase of grief is depression, which I believe is the phase you are in currently. You are feeling low because the world as you knew it has been turned upside down. You are trying to adapt to your new reality and as you miss your parents, you are feeling displaced, unloved, emotionally unstable and questioning the purpose of life. I'm here to help you process this and hopefully guide you towards the last phase, which is acceptance. Acceptance doesn't mean forgetting your parents; it is just coming to terms with your loss.'

Tiffany nodded. It was a relief to hear that she wasn't having a mental breakdown and the grief she was feeling was a normal progression.

'I have a task I would like to set for you. I'd like you to write letters to your parents telling them of your tears and triumphs. Let them know your thoughts and feelings. It will make you feel less disconnected and will give you an outlet to share any emotions that are weighing you down.'

'Where do I send these letters? I'm pretty sure there's no post office in heaven,' Tiffany replied sarcastically.

'You keep them and then when the time is right, I want you to visit a place that has special significance to you all and then you can burn them, setting your words and emotions free.'

The idea of writing letters to her dead parents made Tiffany feel awkward, but there would be no harm in trying if it helped her reach the elusive level of acceptance.

'I would also like you to practice relaxation techniques of deep breathing and meditation. If you can calm yourself enough to get a decent night's sleep, you will find that you will emotionally cope better the next day. No one deals well with life when they are constantly tired and grumpy. I prefer to get my clients to relax naturally rather than take sleeping tablets.'

'Okay,' Tiffany responded, accepting some printed sheets with relaxation techniques displayed.

'I would like to see you once a week to discuss your feelings in greater depth. Under normal circumstances, people your age are at a crossroads in their lives, having to choose a career path, starting university and adjusting to being adults. You have all that to deal with, but have to do it without the support network of your parents, plus you have the added responsibility of looking after your parents' estate. It would be a trying time for any person. You need to know that you still do have a support network and I will be here to help you as much as I can.'

'Thank you,' Tiffany replied. It gave her a small sense of relief to know that Dr Flanders had dealt with others in this situation and that she was there to act as a confidential sounding board.

CHAPTER 7

With her Dad's favourite fountain pen poised, Tiffany began to write her first letter to her deceased parents:

Dear Mum and Dad,

It's been almost five months since I last got squished between the two of you in a 'Tiffany Sandwich'. I used to think it was childish, but now I would give anything in the world to find myself wedged between the two of you again. I took for granted the love and affection we shared and I miss it so much.

I've started university at Macallister and I'm living on campus. It's pretty basic, but I've made some nice friends and I'm enjoying my courses. I'm particularly interested in my law degree and constantly pick my lecturer's brain over what will happen with your court case. It is due to be heard in August. I saw the guy that caused the accident a few weeks ago and I went and abused him, before having a full-on emotional breakdown in front of the entire uni. I think I will cope better once we know how he will pay for his crime. I honestly feel like he deserves to get life in prison, but my professor says that there is a maximum sentence of 30 years. I'm meeting with the solicitor next week with Uncle Alex to discuss how the case is going.

I got some tattoos. I know you guys don't like them but they are special to me as they remind me of you. I'm sure if you saw them you would think they are tasteful.

I've started seeing a psychiatrist and she has been helpful. In fact, it is her idea that I write to you. I think it makes me seem insane, but I guess it is the opposite since she has recommended it and she is the expert.

Mum, in a few weeks, I'm going to spend your birthday in Noosa with Aunty Jody. She says we have to have a girl's weekend away as she doesn't have a daughter to do those types of things with. I think it will be good for us to have a change of scenery and to celebrate your birthday. I will have a mojito in your honour.

Dad, you'll be happy to know that I'm using your favourite pen to write this letter. It makes me feel a bit closer to you, knowing that your fingers used to wrap around the pen where mine are now resting.

I hate the fact that you two will never get to see me graduate, get married or have kids. You would have made amazing grandparents. I promise I will keep your memory alive and tell my kids all about

you guys.
    I love and miss you both so much.
    Tiff xx

Folding the notepaper in thirds, Tiffany stuffed the letter into an envelope and sealed it before placing it in a box of her treasured possessions in the back of the wardrobe. Although the concept of writing to deceased people had seemed weird, Tiffany felt like a weight had been lifted off her shoulders. It almost felt as if she had sat down with her parents at the dinner table and recounted her day.

CHAPTER 8

Sitting in her one and only suit, opposite the Director of Public Prosecutions, Tiffany felt anxious. She hoped the solicitor would confirm that the evidence was so strong that the case would be over and done in no time and that Harley Jefferson would get the maximum sentence. The arch-lever folder containing reports from the police, hospital and morgue was bulging with paperwork.

The lawyer addressed most of the conversation to Alex, occasionally casting a cursory glance in Tiffany's direction. Most of the discussion was in legalese, a language Tiffany was only just starting to grasp through her university lectures.

'So, Tiff, they have forensic reports that prove Mr Jefferson was driving, that he had been drinking alcohol and that his lack of judgment was the sole cause of the accident,' Alex said, trying to put things in laymen's terms for Tiffany.

'Good, so he should get the maximum sentence then,' Tiffany responded confidently.

The lawyer interjected, 'Not necessarily. The

defence will use the defendant's clean criminal and driving record as leverage. His blood alcohol reading was not high range, which will also have a bearing. We also expect his age will be taken into consideration when sentencing.'

'So, how long do you think he will get for killing three people?' Tiffany asked bluntly.

'I can't say,' the lawyer responded ambiguously. 'I would like you and your aunty to do Victim Impact Statements that may be presented to the judge for consideration if he is convicted.'

'I can help you write that,' Alex said to Tiffany.

'I am also trying to subpoena a friend of the defendant who was drinking with him the night of the accident, to prove he knowingly chose to drive even though he was over the limit. We have to prove he was culpable, not just negligent.'

Tiffany's mind was spinning. She had covered the definitions of culpable versus negligent in a lecture a few weeks prior and she had memorized their definitions, at the time not realising the relevance they would have in her life.

'Would it help the case if we got character references for my parents?' Tiffany asked, clutching at straws to ensure Harley Jefferson paid the time for the crime.

'Unfortunately, the law only looks at facts. Even if he had been responsible for killing ex-cons, the judge will only take into consideration that three lives were lost. There isn't a greater sentence because the people killed were nice.'

Tiffany blushed at her naivety. She thought it did matter that the world was a lesser place for having lost two of the kindest people who ever lived, but the law was black and white. It was about facts, not emotions.

Sitting at her small desk with her laptop open, Tiffany stared at the blank screen. The small flashing black line blinked at her in readiness for her to start typing her victim impact statement. She slammed the lid shut and pushed the computer aside. She reached for a pen and paper and began to scribble furiously.

Dear Mum and Dad,

LIFE SUCKS!

I had an appointment with the solicitor today. He doesn't seem confident that the guy responsible for killing you will get the maximum sentence. He has asked me to write a victim impact statement to help with sentencing if the driver is convicted.

I sat down to write it but how can an accumulation of meaningless words really sum up who you were and what I've lost now that you're gone?

Mum, how can I describe that you were happy without showing them the little crinkles that formed in the corner of your eyes and the way your nose scrunched up ever so slightly when you laughed? How can they understand how brave and protective you were of us, Dad, without knowing you once ran into the front yard in your underpants holding a rolling pin when you could see a group of guys trying to steal our garden hose? A simple typed word on a page doesn't convey the lives and personalities that have been snuffed out by one person's careless actions.

A knock on the door jolted Tiffany out of her memories and back to the present. She turned her letter face down on the desk and opened the door. Standing on the other side was Gabby with arms outstretched.

'Oh my God, what are you doing here?' Tiffany asked, throwing her arms around her best friend.

Gabby had moved to Bathurst to start university, which meant she was several hours' drive away. Tiffany had felt almost abandoned by her at a time when she needed her most, but she knew she couldn't have asked Gabby to postpone university for her selfish needs.

'I missed you,' Gabby responded, hugging Tiffany tightly and rocking her side to side.

'Oh, I've missed you too, Babe. Welcome to my humble home,' Tiffany said, waving her arm around to encompass the pitifully small dorm room.

'I love what you've done with the place,' Gabby

replied sarcastically. Tiffany looked around at the bare brick walls, the plain doona covering her bed and her cluttered desk.

'Yeah, maybe I should be majoring in interior design,' Tiffany replied laughing. 'So, tell me why you are really here.'

'I knew you had the appointment with the solicitor today and I thought you would need a friend. It's not the same Snapchatting and texting on Instagram. Tell me how it went.'

'It was okay. The solicitor is a bit painful. You'd think he was representing the defence with the way he suggested the reasons why the driver should get a light sentence. He wants me to write a victim impact statement but I just can't seem to come up with the words to convey what an impact the death of my parents has had on me.'

'You're great at writing essays. Just think of it like a uni assignment. You will be fine,' Gabby said supportively.

'I guess,' Tiffany replied unconvincingly. 'Anyway, what have you been up to at your uni?'

'O Week was awesome. I think I had a hangover for the entire week. There are some cool people that live in my college. We are in small cottages, so it's not the same as here, but they are homely. I must admit my room is a bit more impressive than this.'

'Anything would have to be a bit more impressive than this,' Tiffany replied, looking glum.

'I walked past your common room and it looks cool. I saw there is a ping-pong table. I assume you play beer pong there?'

'Some of the residents do. I just go down for meals and the rest of the time I stay locked up in here. I'm not great company these days. I've got a few nice friends, but after I had a meltdown on the first night of O Week, I think most people here are scared to talk to me in case I freak out again.'

'How are you coping? You sound miserable,' Gabby said, wrapping an arm around Tiffany's shoulders.

Tiffany burst into tears. 'Honestly, I hate my life. I have so much stress with the workload for a double degree, plus I'm trying to cope with the loss of my parents and deal with the court case. I sometimes think it would have been better if I had been in the car with Mum and Dad and died too.'

'Babe, you have so many people who love and care for you. I know that I don't live around the corner anymore, but I'm only ever a phone call away.'

'I know and I've been seeing a psychiatrist to help. It's just that it is all so overwhelming. It's enough of a huge leap to start uni and live away from home for the first time, without having to deal with the grief of becoming an orphan.' Tiffany reached out to grab a tissue before wiping her eyes and throwing it into a bin that was almost overflowing with discarded tissues. She wondered how many tears the human body could cry until it became a shrivelled up shell.

'Tiff, I think you are doing a great job. I know life isn't easy and you are probably feeling lonely since I've moved away and your parents aren't here anymore, but you are so strong. Hang in there, Babe. You know your parents would be so proud of you.'

Tiffany sniffed as she nodded her head in acceptance. 'I'm so glad you're here, Gab, I've missed you so much.'

'I was thinking we should go down to Manly and grab some fish and chips tonight, just like old times. What do you think?' Gabby asked.

'That's a perfect plan. Let me just put on a mask of makeup. I don't want to walk around scaring small children when they look at my tear-stained face.'

CHAPTER 9

The weekend had arrived for Tiffany and her Aunty Jody to go away to celebrate her mum's birthday. Tiffany finished packing and then sat on the top of her small carry-on suitcase in an effort to close the zipper. A weekend in the sunshine of Noosa was exactly what both she and her aunty needed to relax and unwind.

Jody had spared no expense and soon Tiffany found herself in awe, sitting next to her aunty in the back seat of a stretched limousine. 'I feel so posh,' Tiffany said, surveying the soft leather seats and the LED lit mini-bar to the side. 'I can't even reach the other seat if I stretch out. Thank you so much. This is so cool.'

'This weekend is all about celebrating your mum. We've had enough tears over the past six months and now it is time to celebrate how lucky we both were to have your mum in our lives,' Jody said, passing Tiffany a glass of champagne.

'Cheers,' Tiffany said, clinking her plastic champagne flute against her aunty's.

'To Sandy,' Jody replied.

'To Mum,' Tiffany responded, 'and to no tears this weekend.'

The tiny bubbles from the French champagne tickled Tiffany's palette. It was a dry wine, much drier than the cheap sweet sparkling wine she had previously drunk with friends.

'Thank you for organising this weekend.' Tiffany smiled. 'I'm looking forward to spending this time with you.' Even though Jody was her mum's younger sister, she could have passed for her twin, except her hair was a shade darker and her lips a bit thinner. Her presence couldn't replace the hole in Tiffany's heart but there was comfort in being with her.

'It's my pleasure, Honey; you are like the daughter I never had. I'm equally excited to be going away with you. Just think; we have three days of no plans. We can sip cocktails in a bar, stroll along the beach or laze around a pool in the warmth of Noosa. It certainly beats the cooler weather we have in Sydney in June.'

Walking into their hotel suite, Tiffany's breath caught at the view out the window that looked across the pool to the beach on the other side of the road. There were vacant cane sun lounges by the pool and waiters walking idly around the area serving guests.

'Time to try out the new bikini I bought you,' Jody said, pulling a cute swim set out of her bag. Tiffany was touched by her aunty's kindness. It was a similar gesture to something her mum would have done.

'Thanks, Aunty Jody, it's gorgeous,' Tiffany said, reviewing the burnt orange bikini.

'I wish I had the body to wear something like that these days. I had so much pleasure in choosing it for you. I know it will look amazing.'

'I'll try it on now,' Tiffany replied. 'I think those sun lounges by the pool have our names on them.'

Tiffany walked out from her room wearing her new swimsuit. 'You look gorgeous, you are the spitting image of your mum at the same age,' Jody said, tears welling in her eyes.

'Remember our pact of no crying this weekend,' Tiffany said, hugging her aunty.

Jody took a deep breath. 'You're right. This is a time for celebrating. Let's hit the pool.'

As her skin soaked up the warmth of the sunshine, a feeling of relaxation seeped into Tiffany's body. Jody opened up a novel to read and Tiffany reached for a notepad.

Dear Mum,

Happy birthday. I can't believe you would have been fifty today.

I'm in Noosa with Aunty Jody. It feels weird

being on a family holiday without you and Dad but Aunty Jody is great company.

I have to admit, I haven't felt this relaxed in a long time. We are lying by the pool, sipping cocktails. You would have loved it here.

I have exams for the end of semester over the next few weeks and then during the holidays, Gabby and I are planning on going camping with some of her friends from her uni.

Sarah, who lives in my college dorm, has invited me to go skiing with some friends towards the end of the break, so I'm tossing up whether I will go or not. I have always preferred warm locations, but I feel like I need to push myself to be social or I will end up as a hermit.

I wish you were here so I could give you hugs and kisses and watch you blow out fifty candles.

I love and miss you so much.

Tiff xx

Tiffany put down the pen and notepad. She knew she should be studying, but she couldn't find the motivation to do so.

'What were you writing?' Jody enquired.

'I've been writing letters to my parents. It's a tool the psychiatrist gave me to deal with my grief. I just wrote a quick note to Mum to wish her a happy birthday.'

'That's sweet. You know she loved you so much. Your mum and dad tried so hard to have you. I felt so nervous telling your mum about both my pregnancies with the boys, as I knew she and your dad had been trying to conceive for years. You know she did three rounds of IVF before she finally had you. The first round she had no success. The second round she had three separate implants. The last one took but then she had a miscarriage at around ten weeks. I've never seen her so devastated than at that time. She nearly gave up trying to have a baby. Your dad was really supportive, but it took a toll on both of them. Doing IVF is a really emotional journey and when you go through all that expense, all the painful injections and the invasive procedures, you really have your heart set on giving birth to a baby. Your dad convinced your mum to try one more round of IVF. They harvested three eggs. You were the first embryo implanted and your parents finally got their miracle baby. Your mum was so terrified that she would lose you throughout the pregnancy. The day you were born was the highlight of both your mum and dad's lives. A few years after you were born, they tried for a sibling for you. Your mum had a frozen embryo implanted but she had a miscarriage after the first few weeks. After that, your mum decided she didn't want to do any more IVF and so they decided they were happy to just focus their efforts on you.'

'Of course, I knew I was conceived by IVF, but I had no idea it took them so long to have me. I can't imagine having to go through such an ordeal to have a child. All my friends spend their time actively trying *not* to fall pregnant. It seems so unfair that a loving couple that desperately wanted children had to go through so much heartache. You know they might have thought I was their miracle child, but I'm the truly grateful one because, without their determination, I would never have been born. It would have been so nice to have a sibling, particularly now that I don't have Mum and Dad around anymore, but I can completely understand why Mum decided to give up trying. I don't know if I could do it, I almost faint at the sight of a needle. That is, except one on a tattoo gun.'

'Your mum never liked needles either, but she was so focused on having a baby, she just did what she needed to do. Thankfully, you were the end result. You were the true love of both your parents' lives and they were so proud of the amazing young woman you are. I know they talked about it at your eighteenth birthday party but your mum would always tell me how blessed they were to have you and how they couldn't have asked for a more perfect daughter.'

'You need to stop talking or I won't be able to hold up our pact of no tears this weekend,' Tiffany said, trying to blink away the threatening tears.

CHAPTER 10

Tiffany collapsed into the soft leather lounge and readied herself for her weekly session with Dr Flanders.

'How have you been this week, Tiffany?'

'I have ups and downs, but I feel like I'm finally starting to have more ups than downs,' Tiffany replied, smiling.

'Each week, we have been breaking our sessions down into one emotion. Today, I thought we should talk about loneliness. How are you adjusting to not having the close relationship with your parents anymore?'

'As you suggested, I've been writing to my parents regularly. I find that helpful, but sometimes it does highlight their absence to me. I would give anything in the world to have a real conversation with them. My aunty has been amazing, but she is busy in her own life and as much as she reminds me of my mum, she can't replace her.'

'Every relationship we have is unique. You need to accept and care for your relatives as a separate entity to your parents. What is your relationship like with your uncle?'

'He has been really supportive. He has been helpful in explaining the court case and has been amazing in looking after all the paperwork and bills associated with the estate. I don't think I could have coped with all that on top of everything else.'

'You are very lucky to have such a supportive family. Let me ask you about university. Do you feel living on campus at university makes you feel more or less lonely?'

Tiffany paused to reflect. 'You would think being surrounded by so many people it would be hard to feel isolated, but I lock myself away in my little room and just get on with my work. It's lonely going from living as part of a family to now just being by myself in my room.'

'Have you made friends at uni?'

'Yes, there are a few girls I'm friendly with, but as you can guess, I'm not really the life of the party, and most of the people I live with are there solely to party. It doesn't make me popular to not be involved in social activities. I just find it hard to find any enthusiasm to want to be part of it. When I concentrate on studying, I have to focus so hard that it gives me respite from my feelings. When I have free time, I can't help but dwell on how sad I am to have lost my parents. My greatest escape is to just sleep. At least when you are unconscious, you have no thoughts and feelings.'

'That is all perfectly normal and it takes time to grieve and come to terms with the passing of a loved one. Are you still close with your old school friends?'

'My best friend, Gabby, moved away to uni in Bathurst. We are still in contact and she is a great support but I really miss her. I think it would have been easier to make the transition into my new life if I'd had her by my side.'

'We can't always be in close proximity to friends, but it doesn't mean the friendship is less worthwhile. In fact, some relationships strengthen with distance as you learn to appreciate each other more when you don't take each other for granted. It sounds like Gabby is a special friend. She knew your parents and she would be feeling a level of her own personal grief at their loss as well. Make sure you lean on and support each other. She would understand how you are feeling more than people who never met your parents. Do you have a partner?'

'No, the last thing I need at this point in time is a boyfriend. I'm struggling to just deal with day to day life, without adding another person's feelings into the mix.'

'Do you think you would benefit from doing some sport or recreational activity where you would have social contact with more people?'

'I used to do twilight sailing but ever since my parents died, I've had a recurring nightmare where I'm skippering the boat and my parents are both washed overboard and I can't turn the yacht around. I race off with the spinnaker up and I just leave my parents to die.'

'That's an interesting dream. I would interpret that as a manifestation of the guilt you felt that your parents died when you were having fun. You want to be able to change what happened, but you have to keep moving forward. Do you think that makes sense?'

Tiffany reached for the ever-present box of tissues to blot tears from her eyes. 'That makes perfect sense to me. I do feel guilty. If I'd not been partying, I would have been with them and maybe I could have changed things, or at least I would have died with them.'

'Okay, Tiffany, I want you to do an exercise for homework this week. I want you to say out loud ten times every day, "it's not my fault", "I couldn't have changed things" and "it's okay to have fun". You need to accept that what happened is outside the realm of what you can take responsibility for and you need to start enjoying life again. You can't keep locking yourself away. It doesn't make you a less loving daughter to go out and enjoy socialising with friends. In fact, I think your parents would be devastated if they knew you were so lonely and you weren't living life to the fullest.'

'Okay, but I have exams coming up so I do need to lock myself away to study,' Tiffany said, wiping at her tears with the back of her hand.

'That is totally fine. Please promise me that when you have your holidays in a few weeks that you will make an effort to socialise and have fun.'

Over the following few weeks, the dorms grew quiet as students finally focused on their studies. Everyone had end of semester exams and the students all wore a look of quiet resignation, stress and tiredness.

Tiffany had thrown herself into her studies all term, so while most of her dorm mates were cramming; she was able to simply revise. Although her stress levels were high, she went into her exams knowing that she couldn't have given her course any more of her attention. She felt strangely calm on the morning of her first exam. If there was one thing the previous year had taught her, it was to not sweat the small stuff. The absolute worst case scenario was that she failed and had to do a subject again. It didn't even come close to the stress and pain she felt on a daily basis.

Tiffany systematically ticked off each exam and with the completion of each test, her stress levels eased slightly. Once the last exam was finished, Tiffany packed her bag to join Gabby and her friends camping on a farm. Tiffany had no experience camping – the closest she had ever come to camping was staying on a yacht overnight. She threw jeans, jumpers and gumboots into her duffle bag. It was time to get outside her comfort zone, meeting new people and creating new experiences. She had no idea what the week would hold, but it had to be better than the half-life she had been living for the past six months.

Tiffany pulled up outside the neat brick cottage that Gabby lived in. It looked like a villa in a retirement village. She knocked on the door, half expecting a dear old Grandma to open it. Instead, Gabby flung open the door and threw herself into Tiffany's arms.

'You're finally here. I've missed you, Tiff,' Gabby said.

'It's so good to see you, Gab,' Tiffany replied, choking on tears.

'Come inside and meet my roommates. This is Katie, Rachel and Andrea.'

Tiffany greeted each girl. She had heard snippets about them all from Gabby, so it was good to finally meet them in the flesh.

'We have the car packed and we are ready to go to Katie's parent's farm. It's going to be chilly, so I hope you packed warm clothes.'

Tiffany threw her duffle bag into the boot of

Gabby's car. The three roommates squashed into the back seat of Gabby's old silver Hyundai Getz and Tiffany sat in the front next to Gabby. Within an hour, they had reached the potholed dirt road leading to the farm. A cloud of dust plumed out behind the car. Tiffany jumped out of the car to unlatch the cold metal gate that was the opening to the perimeter fence that surrounded the farm. Once the gate was securely latched once more, the car continued across a cattle grid and drove for another five minutes down the 'driveway'. There were streets in Sydney shorter than Katie's farm's driveway. Tiffany looked at the lush green pastures filled with herds of cows, each with their own unique hide that resembled an inkblot test page. Tiffany reflected that it was good to do something completely different to experiences she'd had with her parents, as there were no painful reminders attached to them.

They eventually drove up alongside a weatherboard clad home with a wide veranda wrapping around the house. Several dogs raced out to greet them, each with their tail wagging, vying for attention from the new arrivals.

'Get down, you mutts,' Katie said good-naturedly to the dogs. A high-pitched whistle from the house saw the dogs immediately turn and run towards the sound.

Katie introduced the group of girls to her parents

and little sister.

'Thank you for having us here,' Tiffany said politely, shaking Katie's dad's hand.

'No problems, Luv. If you get bored, I've got some calves that need castrating,' he said in a broad Australian accent before chuckling.

Tiffany's stomach recoiled. The last thing she wanted to do on holidays was neuter a calf.

'Just ignore him, Tiffany,' Katie said, jabbing her dad in the ribs. It was an action that Tiffany herself had done on many occasions with her dad. An intimate gesture that showed their easy bond, something that Tiffany hadn't even realised she missed with her dad.

'Come on, girls, I thought we could camp down by the creek. We can take our gear there by ATV. We need to get the tents pitched and a fire started before it gets dark,' Katie said, leading the girls to a nearby shed that housed multiple ATVs and motorbikes.

Tiffany and Gabby laughed until tears ran down their faces. They were valiantly trying to pitch their bright yellow tent, but it was a case of the blind leading the blind. Every time they tensioned a rope to a tent post, the tent would lean sideways and buckle in a heap on the ground. The other girls refused to help on the grounds that it was character building and a skill all people should have. They instead collected firewood, while the city girls flailed. Eventually, the tent, although a little lopsided, was pitched and Gabby brought the sleeping bags into the tent and laid them on the ground.

'Where are the mattresses?' Tiffany asked.

'What mattresses?' Gabby responded.

'Are we really sleeping on the cold, hard ground?' Tiffany asked, hoping it was a practical joke.

'Mmm, I hadn't really thought about that. Oh well, think of it as an adventure,' Gabby said collapsing in laughter. 'It's time for us city girls to toughen up.'

'Shotty the side closest to the fire then,' Tiffany said, dumping her clothes on the swag that would be her bed for the next week.

Once Katie had a roaring fire going, the girls sat down on camp chairs and relaxed with a rum and coke. The crackling of the fire, the babbling of the nearby creek and the occasional moo from a cow created a tranquil ambience. Tiffany sipped her drink slowly while the other girls drank insatiably – all of them wanting to unwind after end of semester exams. Ever since the night of her parent's death, Tiffany felt anxious about getting blind drunk just in case there was an emergency.

The more the girls drank, the rowdier they

became. They shared stories about hazing ceremonies they had encountered in their first few weeks at college and their experiences dating at university. Tiffany had nothing to add to the stories, but was happy to be a voyeur soaking up their fun antics.

By midnight, exhaustion began to kick in and the girls crawled into their tents. Tiffany shivered as she shimmied her way into her sleeping bag. The ground was hard under her body, but the few drinks she'd had took the edge off her discomfort.

In the middle of the night, a rustling noise woke Tiffany. She lay still and looked around. Everything was pitch black. Her heart raced wildly.

'Gab, what's that noise?' Tiffany whispered into the darkness.

Tiffany could hear the soft movement of Gabby's breath, indicating she was still fast asleep. Tiffany grabbed her phone and turned on the torch. She mustered all her confidence and then slowly unzipped the front zipper to shine the torch outside. Two demonic eyes stared back at her. 'Shit,' she exclaimed, lurching back into the tent. She noticed the outline of a wallaby before becoming startled. It bounded away, tripping on a tent guy rope, collapsing the tent on top of the girls.

'What the hell?' Gabby said, disoriented with the side of the tent lying across her.

'A wallaby just sabotaged our tent,' Tiffany

laughed while trying to find her way out of the tent to see if she could pitch it again. 'We struggled to put up the tent in broad daylight; I don't know how this is going to go. Can you hold the pole while I try to put the rope on again?' Tiffany asked as she finally found the opening to escape the canvas tomb.

Finally, after ten minutes of scrambling in the dark, the girls managed to get the tent to stay up.

Tiffany crawled back into the tent and the girls giggled, just as they had at sleepovers when they were children.

The first rays of light sent a yellow glow across the inside of the tent. Tiffany stretched; the point of her shoulder and hip ached from lying on the hard ground. Tiffany crawled towards the opening of the tent and stuck her head out to check on whether the other girls had surfaced. A light frost on the grass glistened in the early morning light and gave the area a fresh and almost magical quality.

Tiffany slipped on her shoes and stood to stretch. Although she was sure the girls were still hours from waking, she knew there was no hope of her getting comfortable enough to doze any longer. Sitting on a camp chair, Tiffany sat by the ashes of the night's previous fire and contemplated her life. Last night, the fire had raged with life and had kept them all warm and secure, today, all that was left were the lifeless charred remains – much like her life.

The serenity of the campsite was simultaneously calming and lonely. Tiffany had been trying hard to find closure and come to terms with her parents' death but in certain moments, her grief caught her unaware. Her body ached, but only fractionally less than her heart. She knew she had her whole life ahead of her, but sometimes she struggled to find a reason to live.

The sound of a zipper on a nearby tent roused Tiffany from her morose thoughts. It was time to put on the mask of a fun-loving, confident adult to hide the scared, lonely child she was.

Katie appeared, squinting into the bright morning sun.

'How did you sleep?' Katie asked.

'Apart from a wallaby sabotaging our tent in the middle of the night, and having no mattress, I slept well.'

Katie laughed. 'Well, if it's any consolation, I've got a cracking headache. Having a hangover, makes you wonder whether it's worth partying the night before.'

'The first night is always the biggest. What's on the agenda for today?' Tiffany asked, prodding the ashes of the fire.

'I thought we could go for a float down the creek. There are rapids a bit further down.'

'What will we float on?' Tiffany asked, looking around the campsite.

'I've got some tyre inner tubes and inflatable mattresses we can use.'

'Did you just say you have inflatable mattresses? Like the ones that you can lie on comfortably to sleep on, rather than just lying on the hard ground?' Tiffany asked incredulously.

Katie looked sheepish. 'Yep, I've got three of them in a crate in the back of the ATV. I'm sorry it didn't occur to me that you and Gabby could have used them last night. I promise they are all yours from now on.'

The days of camping passed in a whirlwind of drinking, playing games, horse riding and roasting marshmallows. Having fun together distracted Tiffany from her grief, but Tiffany knew that a wave of sorrow was only ever a short distance away, ready to wash over her as soon as she was alone once again.

CHAPTER 11

As soon as Tiffany returned from her camping trip, her focus returned to the looming court case for her parents. She wrote and edited her victim impact statement multiple times. The words never seemed enough to relay her true emotions. Eventually, she had to submit a statement and make peace with the fact that a heartfelt outpouring of emotions was the closest she would get to summarising the impact the accident had on her life.

On the morning of the court case, Tiffany awoke to the sound of light rain. It seemed fitting to have bleak weather on such a miserable day. A grey haze filtered through the window as Tiffany dressed in plain black pants and a white collared shirt. She wanted to appear respectful in her attire and didn't have a wide range of clothes. With the allowance from her inheritance, she knew she could have bought a whole new wardrobe of clothes, but she lacked the motivation to go shopping.

Sydney's streets were slick from rain, random puddles created obstacles for the crowds trying to navigate their way to office blocks without being drenched. Running through the streets of the city, huddled under a compact umbrella, Tiffany began to feel anxious about the case ahead. She had been briefed on possible outcomes and was worried that Harley Jefferson would walk away unscathed.

As Tiffany shook the water droplets from her umbrella, she spied her aunty and uncle with the lawyer, huddled in a corner of the Supreme Court's foyer. They all looked serious, all fully aware of the magnitude of the looming case. The lawyer quietly briefed them on the day's proceedings before they all lined up to go through security. They lay their bags and dripping umbrellas on the conveyor belt to be scanned before walking through a metal detector. Tiffany's heart felt like a lump of lead, but the green lights on the side of the machine did not waiver as she walked through.

The lawyer led them to a wood veneered room, bland in appearance, devoid of personality, the perfect location to focus on the crime at hand. The room was empty with the exception of one man who, too, was bland in appearance in his grey suit and tie.

Within moments, the courtroom began to fill with people. The defence lawyers wheeled in folders of information, Harley Jefferson sat in the dock looking nervous and uncomfortable in a new suit. His parents sat with a girl about Tiffany's age, who had similar colouring to Harley with dark straight hair smoothed down her back. Tiffany, her aunt and uncle took their place in the public gallery seats and the court reporter took her place in front of the typewriter. A buzz of nervous energy filled the room.

Tiffany locked eyes with a middle-aged woman sitting further along the row. She had a vacant look and dark circles under her eyes. Tiffany instantly recognised the expression the woman wore. It was similar to what she saw herself each morning in the mirror. It was the look of grief. The look of someone broken who may never feel whole again. The woman's husband clumsily patted her on the back with one hand, while his other hand nervously raked over his slicked back hair. Without having to be told, Tiffany knew this couple had to be the parents of Tia Mendez, the other victim in the car accident. Tiffany looked away. There was a limit to the amount of grief she could cope with and she had no capacity to deal with their loss on top of her own.

The bland looking man addressed the room. 'All rise.' The scraping of chairs and shuffling of people saw all attendees stand.

'The Supreme Court of NSW is now in session and his Honour Justice Stephen Brooks is now in attendance.'

The justice, sporting a white wig and dressed in a

red gown lined in white fur, took his seat.

Everyone in the courtroom followed his lead and sat. Tiffany leaned over and whispered in her aunty's ear, 'He looks like Santa.' Jody smiled and nodded silently in agreement.

'The case before the court is the Crown vs Jefferson, H. Driving causing Death Section 52A of the Crimes Act 1900. How does the defendant plead?'

Harley Jefferson wiped sweat from his brow. 'Your Honour, I plead not guilty.'

The judge nodded and scribbled a note on the pad in front of him.

The bailiff left the room and after a short interval, he led a group of jurors into the court. Tiffany reviewed them, trying to decipher their personalities and ethics. They ranged in age, sex and ethnicity. Tiffany desperately hoped that when the time came to make their decision, they would all put themselves in her shoes and consider how they would feel if they lost their parents.

When prompted, the prosecutor stood and turned to the jury. 'Ladies and gentlemen of the jury. Today, we are here to make a judgement on whether Mr Harley Jefferson was culpable in causing the deaths of three innocent people. On the evening of the 27th of November 2015, Mr Jefferson attended a party and knowingly consumed alcohol before deciding to drive his girlfriend, Tia Mendez, home. At 12.15am, driving along Pittwater Road, Brookvale; Mr Jefferson lost control of the car he was driving and ran into a stationary car waiting at traffic lights, driven by Mr David Parker and with a passenger, Mrs Sandra Parker. The result of the accident was the death of three innocent parties: Ms Mendez and Mr and Mrs Parker. Mr Jefferson suffered minor cuts and abrasions. He returned a blood alcohol concentration reading of 0.07, that is 0.02 over the legal limit. Had it not been for his reckless behaviour, these three people would still be alive. Ms Mendez would be completing her schooling, with her whole future ahead of her and Mr and Mrs Parker's only child would not now be orphaned. I will be calling upon police forensic records and medical reports to give you the facts. We will establish without a doubt that Mr Jefferson is guilty of culpable driving, resulting in three deaths and it is your duty as the jury to ensure he is penalised for his actions.'

Tiffany watched the reactions of the jurors. Some looked aghast at the facts; others sat with neutral expressions. The prosecutor sat and the barrister for the defence stood.

'Good morning, Jurors. My client, Mr Harley Jefferson, is a twenty-year-old university student. He is a good kid with great grades, training to be a teacher. He has a clear traffic record and no police record. He is just your average guy. In October 2015, he gained his full licence – the first time in his driving experience that he was allowed to consume any alcohol. It is a tricky thing to judge when you've had an amount of alcohol that would be under the 0.05 limit. I'm sure I don't only speak for myself when I say that it is always guesswork estimating what your blood alcohol level would be. It is not an exact science. Your reading can change based on your sex, body type and time between drinks, some people can drink two standard drinks and be over the limit, while others will be under the limit after 5 drinks. Mr Jefferson is guilty of not correctly estimating what his blood alcohol limit would be. His reading is considered low range and, under normal circumstances, he would lose his licence for six months and receive a fine.

Unfortunately, on the morning of the 15ᵗʰ of November 2015, Mr Jefferson had a lapse in judgement when driving. He was tired and as a relatively inexperienced driver, remember, he only has three years driving experience, he misjudged a corner and hit a car sitting stationary at a set of lights. The tragic consequence of Mr Jefferson's inexperience was that three people lost their lives. Mr Jefferson is remorseful and while the accident didn't leave many external marks on him, Mr Jefferson will have to deal with the emotional turmoil of his actions for the rest of his life. That in itself is a tough sentence. I ask you to take a look at the defendant. He isn't a drug-fuelled felon, he is just like the boy next door. He deserves to have a bright future and take a leadership role in helping mentor our next generation of children once he is a qualified teacher. There was no culpability in this accident; it was just the result of inexperience. Mr Jefferson made a mistake. That makes him human, not a criminal. I humbly ask that you take into consideration his age, lack of driving experience and his clean police record when you have a recess to make your decision. Thank you.'

Tiffany's gaze drifted over to Harley Jefferson. His face was red, blushing from the attention. Looking meek and humble, he wiped sweat from his brow once more. Listening to the barrister, Tiffany had almost felt sympathy for Harley's predicament. If he had been one of her friends and she hadn't lost her parents, would she have been so keen to see him incarcerated? Tiffany felt sick with dread. If the jurors were swayed into thinking he was an upstanding citizen, he may never receive the level of justice her parents deserved.

Being in court was a tiring experience. Day after day, new witnesses were called to give evidence. Each small shift in momentum towards their case saw the defence counteract it. After six days of evidence and argument, Tiffany did not have a clear indication as to which way the jury would sway. She was relieved when the jury was finally sequestered for deliberations as at least a result would be imminent and she could finally get some closure.

Tiffany sat opposite her aunty and uncle in a local café. The cheap vinyl seat she had chosen to sit on had a small rip in it that had snagged her stockings. As she freed her stocking from the vinyl, she watched the small ladder creep up her leg. Alex leant forward and the laminate table rocked back and forth like a drunkard trying to appear stable. With her nerves already fried, these minor irritations that would normally not faze Tiffany were blown out of proportion.

'For God's sake, we don't live in a third world country. Why can't these people get decent furniture?' Tiffany ranted.

Alex and Jody locked eyes. The strain was clear. They were all on edge awaiting the court's decision. The minutes passed slowly. Time had a way of slowing when you were desperate to know an outcome.

'Well, I have no idea what the verdict will be,' Alex said, stirring his coffee.

'They made out Harley Jefferson was a saint. I wouldn't be surprised if after this court case he gets knighted,' Tiffany scoffed.

'Tiff, keep in mind that everyone on that jury has a family. I think the evidence you and Mrs Mendez gave was very emotive. There was barely a dry eye in the house. It will be hard for people to simply forgive his actions,' Jody added, the voice of calm in the storm of emotions.

'The real question is whether they have proved that he was culpable. The sentences for culpable driving versus dangerous driving are poles apart,' Alex added.

'Waiting for the jury's decision is unbearable. I just want to know what the outcome is so that we can move on with our lives,' Tiffany said, her leg nervously twitching with anxiety.

'I think the most important thing about this court case is that it will help bring closure. Whatever the result, we know that the legal process has been upheld and that's all we can really ask for,' Jody said calmly.

Tiffany took a deep breath and, tapping her fingers on the laminate tabletop, addressed her uncle, 'How long until there is a decision?'

'How long is a piece of string? It could take an hour or three days.'

'I can't sit here any longer. The stale air, the vile coffee and crappy furniture are driving me insane. I'm going to go for a walk. Please let me know if the court is recalled.'

Tiffany walked across the road into Hyde Park, her nervous energy finding its release as she strode quickly along the concrete path. She watched people running, seeking their own release from work stresses; a homeless man lying beneath a tree, wrapped in a dirty old grey blanket and Asian tourists posing with selfie sticks in front of the fountain. Each person a welcome distraction – a way to avoid watching the second hand on her watch that seemed to move too slowly.

Sitting on a park bench, Tiffany shivered. She wasn't sure if it was from the cold or nerves. Her phone vibrated in her pocket. A text from Gabby: **how are things going?**

No news

Let me know the result when you get it

Tiffany's phone buzzed again, this time a text from Jody. *Come back to the courthouse, the jury is ready.*

On my way.

Tiffany walked briskly towards the courthouse, keen to learn the judgement she had been nervously awaiting.

Alex, Jody and Tiffany entered the courtroom, bowing in deference as they had each day of the trial.

The jury was already seated and Tiffany searched their faces for any sign of the verdict.

Harley Jefferson was brought into the courtroom and sat with his head bowed, his hands nervously drummed on his thighs, his anxiety clear for all to see.

'All rise. The Supreme Court of NSW is now in session and the honourable Justice Stephen Brooks is now in attendance.'

Everyone in the court was quiet as they rose for the judge's entrance.

'Be seated. The case before the court is the Crown vs Jefferson, H. Driving causing Death Section 52A of the Crimes Act 1900. I call upon the foreperson of the jury. Has the jury agreed upon a verdict?'

'We have, your Honour. We find the defendant guilty.'

Tiffany expelled the breath she hadn't realised she had been holding.

'Thank you, jurors. The jury is now excused. Bail is revoked and the defendant, Mr Harley Jefferson, will be remanded in custody. Court is adjourned until 16th August 2016 at 9am, when I will hand down the sentence after considering the submission.' Justice Brooks then rose and swiftly exited the courtroom.

Tiffany smiled as she watched Harley Jefferson being handcuffed and led out of the room, feeling a sense of satisfaction that justice had been served. Tiffany watched as Harley's father tried to console his mother who wept uncontrollably. Tiffany felt no pity for them. His mother's tears were only a fraction of the tears Tiffany had cried. It wasn't as if her son had actually been killed like her parents had.

Once they exited the courtroom, Tiffany hugged her aunty. Tears of joy ran unchecked down their cheeks. 'We did it,' Tiffany said. 'I'm so relieved the jury agreed he was guilty.'

'It won't bring back your parents, but at least justice has been served,' Jody said. She held Tiffany at an arm's distance. 'We are so proud of you. You were so brave to stand up in the courtroom and give evidence.'

'Thanks, Aunty Jody.'

The prosecutor for the Crown contacted Tiffany. 'If you want to read your victim impact statement to the judge prior to sentencing, it will need to be done this afternoon. It is not compulsory so it is completely up to you.'

Tiffany stood in the witness box in front of the judge. The room was eerily quiet.

'My name is Tiffany Parker. The 26ᵗʰ of

November 2015, was the best day of my life. I
turned eighteen and I celebrated with my family and
friends. At my party, my dad gave a heart-warming
speech about how proud my parents were of me.
Being an only child, I was extremely close to my
mum and dad. I couldn't have asked for better
parents. They were loving, supportive, caring,
devoted, intelligent human beings. It took them a lot
of heartache and pain to conceive me and so I knew
without a doubt that I was loved and cherished. I
was their miracle child. I never doubted how
blessed I was. I was their world and they were mine.

'The 27ᵗʰ of November 2015, was the worst day
of my life. It was the day a reckless drunk driver
killed my parents, my only immediate family. They
were simply sitting at a set of traffic lights coming
home from my party, when Harley Jefferson
ploughed his car into their stationary car. In that
moment, he stole from me not only my parents but
also my best friends. After everything it took for my
parents to have me, they will now not see me
graduate university, they won't be there to give me
away at my wedding nor live to see their
grandchildren.

'I am now lost and alone. An orphan. I have had
the most important people in the world to me taken
away due to the reckless behaviour of one man. He
gets to live at home with his parents, he gets their
unconditional support, he gets to live his life in a

way that I will never be able to.

'I have had to seek counselling from a psychiatrist to try to help me deal with the insurmountable grief that Mr Jefferson's careless actions have caused. Until the day I die, I will never be able to come to terms with their senseless deaths.'

Tiffany sobbed as tears cascaded down her cheeks and off her chin, leaving small water marks on her blouse. She took a moment to try to calm herself.

With her chin wobbling, Tiffany continued, 'everyone should have the right to grow up with their parents there supporting them. I have had that stolen from me. I will always love my parents but I can no longer laugh with them, talk to them, hug or kiss them. I have a giant gaping hole in my heart that I don't think will ever feel normal again. This darkness and despair is solely the responsibility of one person, Mr Harley Jefferson.'

Judge Brooks looked at Tiffany. 'Thank you, Ms Parker. I am sorry for your loss and I appreciate you sharing your statement.'

The morning of the 16th of August, Jody, Alex and Tiffany entered court to hear the sentence for Harley Jefferson be handed down. After the normal routine of announcing the judge, everyone sat with bated breath awaiting the penalty.

Judge Brooks, dressed in his white wig and red fur-lined cape, peered at Harley Jefferson over the top of his spectacles.

'Today is the sentencing hearing of the case of the Crown vs Jefferson, H. Driving causing Death Section 52A of the Crimes Act 1900. As unanimously agreed by the jury on 12th August 2016, Mr Harley Jefferson was found guilty of driving causing death. In sentencing, all evidence was considered. Ms Parker and Mrs Mendez both presented a Victim's Impact Statement to me and it is clear that this accident has had a profound effect on them both.' Tiffany nodded silently.

'It has been demonstrated that Mr Jefferson is an upstanding citizen, with no prior criminal convictions nor any previous driving offences. His youth and inexperience were all key factors that led to the accident on 27th November 2015, which resulted in the deaths of Tia Mendez, Sandra Parker and David Parker. Whilst the deaths of three people is a very serious matter, I do not believe that Mr Jefferson was guilty of culpable driving; that is, he did not knowingly drive in a manner he deemed dangerous. The evidence showed that Mr Jefferson was not speeding when he turned the corner, prior to losing control of the car. It also indicated that Mr Jefferson's blood alcohol level was low range and whilst it was his responsibility to ensure he did not drink too much, his testimony stated that he did not feel inebriated and as such, his inexperience led him to incorrectly guess that he would be okay to drive.

'I have taken into consideration the mental anguish that Mr Jefferson will have to deal with for the rest of his life due to this incident. I have also given consideration to the age of Mr Jefferson and the fact that he has shown remorse for his actions.

'The sentence acknowledges the seriousness of the crime, the impact on the families and the unlikely risk of Mr Jefferson re-offending. Furthermore, the sentence is in line with other cases with a similar precedence.

'I hand down the sentence as follows:

-    2-year prison sentence, to be suspended subject to a good behaviour bond. Mr Jefferson will be on home detention and must abide by all the covenants of the bond.
-    2-year disqualification from driving.
-    20-hour driver safety course.
-    A Drug and Alcohol Awareness standard course.

A look of pure relief washed over Harley's face. He nodded eagerly and smiled widely at his parents in the dock.

Tiffany's mouth was agape. She was totally shocked by the sentence. Harley Jefferson was getting a slap on the wrist. Killing three people had resulted in him getting two years to practice his PlayStation skills at home.

Tiffany turned her head to see the same look of outrage on her aunty's face. Jody shook with rage. They had all assumed there would at least be a prison sentence for the crime committed, but the judge had swallowed the defence's propaganda and had decided upon the minimum sentence.

The court proceedings wrapped up in a blur. Tiffany couldn't concentrate on anything else once the sentence had been handed down. Her anger was palpable and she felt so stupid at her premature celebration of the guilty verdict.

Leaving the court, journalists thrust their microphones and cameras in Tiffany's face.

'How do you feel about the sentence?'

'Do you have anything to say to Mr Jefferson?'

'Do you think the sentence is too lenient?'

'Are you going to ask the DPP to appeal?'

For the first time in her life, Tiffany was speechless. Alex stepped in front of her to guard her from the throng of media. 'We have no comment,' he said, fighting his way through the crowd.

As Harley Jefferson exited the court with his parents and the girl Tiffany assumed was his sister, the swarm of media hovered around him. His barrister had prepared a speech. Standing on the footpath outside the court, Harley Jefferson smiled smugly as his barrister addressed the media. 'This has been a harrowing experience for my client. He is remorseful for the deaths caused by his inexperience. He is grateful that the legal system has recognised his exemplary behaviour and clean criminal record. Whilst he may avoid time in prison, he has a life sentence of guilt for his actions. Mr Jefferson understands the gravity of this sentence and will fulfil his requirements. Mr Jefferson looks forward to completing his teaching degree so he can start giving back to society by helping to educate our next generation. We ask now that you give Mr Jefferson and his family privacy to move forward. There will be no further comments. Thank you.'

CHAPTER 12

Sinking into the familiar leather couch, Tiffany struggled to articulate her anger to Dr Flanders. 'I just feel like punching someone,' she hissed through a clenched jaw.

'You need to be able to learn to accept things that are not within the realms of your ability to change.'

'I think I should drop out of my law degree. What's the point of doing law when the system doesn't work?'

'That seems like a drastic measure. I wouldn't make any decisions about university at the moment when you are in a heightened emotional state. Take some time to let things settle down first. You seem a bit agitated today. I really think it would be worthwhile to get you to calm down before we proceed. I would like you to do some breathing exercises with me for a few minutes.'

Together, they went through a deep breathing exercise and Tiffany felt her anger subside slightly.

'Tell me what makes you feel angriest about the

court case.' Dr Flanders said.

'He got off scot-free. It's like my parents' lives were meaningless.'

'Do you believe your parents' lives were meaningless?'

'Of course not. They were the most amazing people ever.'

'Okay. Do you feel like there was any further evidence that could have been used that would have changed the outcome?' Dr Flanders quizzed.

'No. All the evidence I know of was presented, otherwise, we could have pushed for a retrial.'

Dr Flanders nodded. 'Right. As much as you don't like the sentence, he was proven guilty for the crime. He will now have a criminal record for the rest of his life. Would having him sit in a cell for a few years make a difference to your life at all?'

Tiffany sat quietly contemplating the question. In a quiet voice, she answered, 'I guess not. But it still doesn't seem fair.'

'No sentence would have changed your reality. Your lovely parents are not coming back. All you can do now is accept that the legal system has done its job and you need to move forward. It's not healthy to harbour anger because it is non-productive. Stressing about the sentence is only going to ruin your life. You've already suffered enough. It's time to release the stress and anger attached to the accident, accept you can't change what's happened and focus on your future. You can't change the past. You have to live in the present.'

Tiffany nodded numbly. She knew Dr Flanders was right, but it was hard to ignore her feelings of injustice.

'How have you been going with your sleep? Are you still getting nightmares?'

'I didn't sleep well during the court case. A few times I've had the recurring nightmare of me leaving my parents in the water while I sail off into the distance.'

'Would you like a prescription for some sleeping tablets?'

'No. I think it will be better now that the case is finished. As much as I'm angry about the result, I am relieved that it is over.'

'I'm glad you feel that way, Tiffany. Are you still writing letters to your parents?'

'Yes. It definitely helps me to feel closer to them.'

'That's great. You can keep doing that for as long as you want. Also, don't forget that you can also go to visit their graves. Talk to them and share your thoughts and feelings with them while you are there.'

Tiffany hadn't visited her parents' graves for several months, so upon leaving Dr Flander's room, she drove directly to the cemetery.

As Tiffany approached the graves, she noticed flowers that didn't seem too old. Although she hadn't been visiting her parents' graves, it was clear that someone had. The familiar feeling of guilt crept in. She had been so self-absorbed, trying to drag her way through her grief that she hadn't tended to her parents' graves. She knew instinctively that Jody was responsible for caring for her sister's grave. Tiffany replaced the old flowers with the fresh bunch she had brought. She then sat between the matching headstones, a hand on each, a conduit to connect the two cool, smooth marble slabs.

'I'm sorry I've haven't been here much. I wanted to just come check in.' Tiffany began to cry. After a few minutes of surrendering to her tears, she calmed down.

'I'm so sorry that the guy responsible for killing you hasn't gone to jail. We tried everything we could to help the case. If it makes any difference, he was found guilty. I'm really struggling to come to terms with it because it is so wrong that he hasn't been locked up for life, considering he took three lives. My psychiatrist says that I just have to accept it and move on. I know that you want me to live a happy life and so I'm going to try to use that as my motivation to find closure.

'I've been writing letters to you both. I secretly hope that your spirits are just hovering over my shoulder watching and that I've been able to keep you up to date with my thoughts. I had a nice time camping a few weeks ago. I know you're probably giggling at the thought of a city girl like me camping.'

Tiffany sat quietly for a few moments, reflecting on the holidays they had shared as a family.

Choking back tears once more, Tiffany plucked at blades of grass next to the graves. 'I miss you guys so much. Life is never going to be the same without you.'

Tiffany was so engrossed in her discussion with her parents that she hadn't noticed an approaching figure.

'Sorry to interrupt.'

Tiffany squealed in fright. She turned to see the silhouette of a man standing over her. It took her a moment to realise it was Harley Jefferson standing above her, a bunch of flowers in hand.

'What are you doing here? Aren't you supposed to be locked up in your house?' Tiffany said acidly.

'I can travel within a 10km radius from my home so I can still attend uni and I have special dispensation to visit the cemetery once a week.' Harley lifted the hem of his pants to reveal a thick black electronic cuff.

'So, it really is just life as normal for you then?' Tiffany responded bitterly.

'Not really,' Harley responded. 'My mum is waiting in the car. I come to visit Tia and your parents' graves every week. Any time I feel sorry for myself, I think of them and their families and it pretty quickly puts things in perspective for me.' He nodded in the direction of the discarded flowers that lay to the side of the graves. 'That's last week's bunch.'

Tiffany was taken aback. She had been certain her aunty was responsible for caring for her parents' graves.

'So, how are you doing?' Harley asked, awkwardly scuffing the toe of his shoe on the grass.

'Not great,' Tiffany responded tersely. 'Particularly since I keep remembering the smug smile on your face when your barrister was talking to the media.'

'That smile wasn't me being smug, it was relief. I thought I was going to be locked away for life. You know that I am truly sorry. I would do anything to change that night.'

Tiffany nodded silently.

'Anyway, I don't want to intrude. It seems you've just left fresh flowers. Why don't you keep these?' Harley thrust the bunch of flowers towards Tiffany. She instinctively grasped them, although she held them out in front of her as embracing them would have seemed traitorous.

Harley turned and walked slowly back towards the car park. His retreating figure brought a mix of emotions to Tiffany. Even though she may have judged him too harshly, he was and would always be the reason her parents were dead.

CHAPTER 13

Arriving at her aunty and uncle's house, the aroma of roast beef made Tiffany's mouth water. Home cooked meals were few and far between these days. The university meals were known to rival airplane food.

'Hello, Lovely,' Jody said, hugging Tiffany fiercely.

'Hi, Aunty Jody. How are you?'

'I'm okay. And you?'

'I'm getting there.'

Alex emerged from the study with his son, Jack, in tow.

'Hi, Tiff,' Jack said as he walked towards the kitchen. 'Time to eat.'

'Hi, Jack,' Tiffany responded, but he was on a mission, absorbed in sneaking mouthfuls of food before Jody had a chance to serve their dinner.

Alex laughed. 'Nothing will come between Jack and his food. How are you?'

'I'm fine thanks.' This lie rolled easily off

Tiffany's tongue these days.

'Come and sit at the dinner table before Jack eats everyone's meals.'

The four of them sat devouring the delicious meal. Conversation swung easily to and fro. Tiffany was glad that her aunty and uncle were such easy company.

'So, guys, we have news,' Jody said, a wide smile broadening across her face. 'We are going on a trip.'

'Where to?' Jack asked, his mouth full of food.

'Well, based on the events of the last year, we have come to the realisation that you can't put off life until you retire. You have to live life to the fullest while you can. We have decided that we are going to hire a motor home and drive around Europe for six months.'

'That's great,' Tiffany responded, plastering a fake smile on her face. In reality, she felt like she was being abandoned once more.

'Cool. Can I come?' Jack asked, grinning.

'If you can get time off work and pay your own way, you are welcome to join us,' Alex replied.

'Forget that,' Jack responded, 'I'd much rather go surfing in Bali than drive around Europe. I'm not a grey nomad.'

'So, when do you leave?' Tiffany asked.

'In three weeks,' Alex replied. 'Tiff, it means

that I won't be able to keep looking after your estate. I'll need to sit down with you and make sure you understand where everything is invested and what you need to do. We've been waiting until after the court case so you would have less stress and would be able to handle it.'

Tiffany had taken for granted the fact that her uncle managed her estate. It hadn't even occurred to her to take over that responsibility. 'No worries.'

Jody continued to talk excitedly about their plans, outlining the countries they would visit and the sights they would see. Tiffany was happy for them, but she secretly felt like crying. She was going to miss them. She felt as if, she would now truly be all on her own.

Seeing Tiffany looking crestfallen, Jody leaned over, 'Are you okay?'

Tiffany wiped an errant tear from her eye, 'I'm just going to miss you.'

'Aww, Tiff. That's so sweet,' Jody said, covering Tiffany's hand with her own. She then turned to Jack, 'Where are your tears, Jack?'

'What tears?' Jack joked, 'I'm already planning a party here.' They all laughed. 'It's okay, Tiff, I'll invite you. You can wear a bikini and be in charge of pouring the drinks.'

Alex playfully swatted the back of Jack's head. 'Boofhead.'

A week later, Tiffany found herself in Alex's wood panelled office. He had folders strewn across the desk, each with a carefully hand-written tab to designate what it contained.

Tiffany found the thought of handling her own affairs daunting, but her uncle was patient and explained everything thoroughly.

'If you have any questions when we are away, you can send me an email and I'll help you if I can. There is a direct deposit of funds that goes into your bank account every month and any recurring bills also get paid directly. I've set up a private mailbox so all mail will go there and you just need to collect it regularly. Do you have any questions?'

Tiffany's mind swum with information, she was sure she would have lots of questions but none of them would come to the surface. 'I just need some time to get my head around this. It should be okay.'

'You'll be fine, Kiddo,' Alex said, packing the folders into an archive box.

Laden down with the cardboard box, Tiffany waddled to her car. It shocked her that her parent's worldly goods had been compressed into sheets of paper that she now struggled to carry.

When Tiffany arrived back at the dorm, a party was in full swing in the communal area downstairs. 'Come join us, Tiff,' Sarah yelled out across the room.

'I've got to put this stuff upstairs,' Tiffany yelled back over the booming music.

'Okay, but if you're not back here within five minutes, I'm going to come and drag you down here myself,' Sarah yelled.

Tiffany placed the box in the bottom of her wardrobe, applied a light smear of lipstick and brushed her hair before returning downstairs. After the stress of the day, some mindless fun was exactly what the doctor ordered.

Walking into the common room, Tiffany could feel the bass beat vibrating through her body. She glanced around the room, trying to spot Sarah. There was a game of beer pong happening on the table tennis table, with raucous laughing and cheering erupting periodically. The lounge had been overtaken by couples with their heads mashed together as they made out, oblivious to the surrounding party. A group of girls danced in a circle, their drinks sloshing out of red plastic cups. Tiffany pitied the cleaners on duty in the morning. There was no sign of Sarah. There was nothing like being surrounded by a hoard of people, but feeling all alone. Tiffany spotted Sunani standing in a small group by the window.

'Hey,' Sunani said, handing Tiffany a drink as she approached.

Although Tiffany tried to avoid drinking, it was

awkward to be stone cold sober amongst a group of drunken people. 'Thanks.'

'I haven't seen you around much. How have you been?' Sunani asked over the thumping bass.

'Okay,' Tiffany replied, nodding her head and sipping her drink. 'Have you seen Sarah?'

'She disappeared with Aaron a few minutes ago.' Sunani grinned and jerked her head in the general direction of the dorm rooms.

'Oh okay. She asked me to join her but it seems like Aaron beat me to it.'

'Come and have a dance with me. I love this song.'

Tiffany reluctantly headed to the makeshift dance floor. The lino underfoot was as sticky as she had imagined.

While drinking with her dorm mates was a welcome distraction, Tiffany was wary about having too much. One drink relaxed her; two drinks made her giggly; three drinks turned her into an emotional mess.

Within an hour, the noise began to wind down as people headed out to the local pub to continue partying.

Tiffany retreated to her bedroom and lay fully clothed on her bed. Reflecting on the night, she knew that she needed to make more of an effort to fit in. She was aware people felt she had wallowed in self-pity for too long. She knew it was time to start moving forward. Her family wasn't coming back, so she would need to make new connections to fill that void.

Looking at the framed family photo of her with her parents on a beach in Fiji, Tiffany made a silent pact that as soon as she had finished her mid-semester exams, she would book a holiday to Fiji and stay in the same resort she had stayed in with her parents. It would be a time for her to cherish the family she would always love while finding closure and the confidence to move on.

CHAPTER 14

'Bula', a smiling Fijian mama greeted Tiffany at the airport before placing a delicate frangipani lei around her neck. Tiffany instantly felt a sense of joy; a homecoming to a place that she held dear. Her senses were overloaded with familiar smells, sights and sounds. The rich aroma of lush tropical undergrowth in the humid air hit her nostrils as she exited the airport to board the transfer bus. Memories flooded back to her as she watched the tropical scenery flash past the windows. The humble houses with cheeky children playing in the yards were haphazardly dispersed amongst the landscape as free-range chickens strutted about.

Finally reaching her destination, Tiffany wandered into the reception area where modern highly polished marble tiles butted up against traditionally carved wooden posts and beams. The receptionist warmly welcomed the group. She was a friendly Fijian lady, wearing a brightly coloured hibiscus print dress, her hair a fuzzy afro, with a white frangipani pinned above her ear. Tiffany eagerly accepted an ice-cold cocktail from her before checking into the resort. As she looked out at the families frolicking in the pool, an all too familiar lump stuck in her throat. The last time she had visited this resort she had been a young teen who had spent her days splashing in the pool while her parents lay in the sun. Such warm memories, contrasted against her current reality. She was alone and it was time to accept it.

After unpacking her suitcase in her neat little tropical bungalow, Tiffany headed down to the beach. The heat and humidity were oppressive and as she dived into the water, she felt she was being cleansed. Not only was she washing away the sticky grime from a day's travel, but for the first time in months, she felt serene and relaxed. She had finally accepted her predicament and was grateful for the wonderful childhood years that she had spent loved and cherished by her parents. As she floated on her back in the calm warm water, looking up at palm trees swaying in the breeze, she had an epiphany that she was finally ready to gain closure.

Walking from the water's edge, Tiffany felt lighter in spirit and knew that she had chosen the right time and place to finally release her pent-up anger and anxiety. It was time to burn the letters she had been writing to her parents, a crutch that she no longer needed. She was keen for them to be burnt to ashes and released on the wind, freeing her of the shackles of her soul-crushing grief.

That evening, Tiffany sat on the grassy foreshore near the beach. She knew from her previous holiday in the resort that each night at sunset, a traditionally dressed Fijian man would perform a torch lighting ceremony, his flame kissing the bamboo torches bringing a row of dancing flames to life along the shoreline.

Sitting in the dusk sunlight, Tiffany read each letter she had written to her parents. The ink on the page wept raw grief and it took her momentarily back to the pain of the time it was penned. After she reflected on each letter, she lit the edge of the page with the flame from the torch, eventually releasing it to be swept away, floating and pirouetting on the wind before disappearing. With every burnt letter, she felt stronger until she finally reached the last letter. She kissed it and said goodbye to her crippling grief before it too turned to ashes.

Tiffany's eyes had adjusted to the fading light and as she turned back to the resort, she was surprised to see it lit up brightly. She could see the unbridled joy in a local Fijian tribe of entertainers who sang and danced in the Polynesian ways of their ancestors. The delight they displayed was only slightly less than the guests who clapped enthusiastically with the music or stood with their phones propped in front of them, capturing the moment to archive the happiness they felt. A young girl was picked from the crowd to learn a traditional dance, much to the delight of her family. Tiffany smiled as she fondly remembered doing the exact same thing on her previous family holiday. She was so proud that she was making headway in no longer being frozen with guilt at remembering happy times. From now on, she would choose to chase happiness and she felt at peace knowing that her parents would want nothing more than for her to enjoy life.

The following morning, Tiffany awoke fresh from a full night's sleep; the nightmares that had plagued her in previous months were now a distant memory. The sun shone through the sheer curtains, bathing her room in a soft golden hue. It was warm but the heat had yet to become stifling. Tiffany stretched and reached for her book. She couldn't remember the last time she had read for pleasure and not for the purpose of making annotations in an essay. She had picked up a light, easy book in the airport bookstore, one that had been advertised as 'perfect holiday reading'. It felt indulgent to lie in bed and take her time to start her day, but as the locals referred to it, she was now on 'Fiji Time', which meant there was no rush.

Her days became full of rest and relaxation, a massage one day, reading by the pool another. No deadlines, no noisy dorm mates, no more mourning. She revelled in watching toddlers floating around the pool with their parents, small kids returning from kid's club proudly producing paintings of palm trees and teenagers Instagramming their mocktails by the pool. She hoped to one day raise a child and bring them back to this resort to experience this little slice of heaven.

On her last day, Tiffany packed her backpack with clothes and rode one of the hotel's complimentary bikes into the local village. She was greeted by little children high-fiving her as she tried to ride. It was quite a task and when she wobbled, the kid's burst into hysterical laughter. Their joy was infectious. She finally stopped her bike and walked towards the teenage girls standing in the back of the group. She held out her clothes to them. She was truly blessed in life and it seemed like such a small gesture to leave some of the local village children with her clothes. The girls giggled and gushed their words of thanks. A village elder invited her inside his home to drink cava, but having heard her father describe it as tasting like mud and making his mouth numb, Tiffany felt it was best to politely refuse the elder's kind offer. As she finally got ready to leave, she rode, with a small army of children running alongside, back to the resort, her backpack and soul feeling lighter from her excursion.

Sitting on the plane on the way home, Tiffany made a 'to-do' list in her phone. For too long, she had been bumbling along. She now felt she had the strength to start setting goals and achieving them. The first thing she wanted to do when she had time was to sort through her parents' belongings. Her Uncle Alex had packed up her family home in order for it to be rented and had put everything in storage. Tiffany knew her parents' clothes and a lot of their possessions would be put to better use going to people in need. She was also sure there were bills being paid for things that were not necessary. Every month, a magazine would turn up addressed to her mum. Tiffany had not wanted to cancel the subscription because she craved things to continue as they always had. What had been sentimental now just seemed wasteful. Tiffany vowed to search through the estate's financials to see where things could be culled. By the time the plane taxied on the runway in Sydney, Tiffany had a long list of jobs to do and a new sense of responsibility.

CHAPTER 15

Tiffany unlocked the roller door to the storage unit and tentatively pushed it up, revealing a room the size of a single garage, packed floor to ceiling with boxes and furniture. She found it odd that a couple's life possessions could be compressed into such a small space. Taking a deep breath, the condensed space smelt like home –
a mixture of her mum's perfume, her dad's aftershave and the scent of the washing detergent in which their clothes had been laundered. They were all smells that Tiffany didn't realise she missed until they assaulted her nostrils, making her grief feel raw once again. Tiffany stepped inside the unit and opened the first box. The moment the cardboard flaps were pushed back, Tiffany was hit by the smell of her mum's scent radiating from the clothes inside. Tears pricked at her eyes. She had thought it would be easy to give away her parents' clothes, but she hadn't expected them to still smell like them. Tiffany pulled her mum's fluffy bathrobe out of the box and, for a few minutes, just stood hugging it

tight to her body. So many mornings she had seen her mum float around the house in the dusky pink robe, preparing lunches and doing chores, mundane tasks that Tiffany had taken for granted. She wished now she had done more to help her mum because the last few months of taking care of herself had been a rude shock. She had never realised how much work her mum did to keep the house running smoothly. After time to reflect, Tiffany pulled herself together and decided she would create a pile of clothes she would keep, either for sentimental reasons or to wear, and a pile to give to charity. The task was taxing but after a few hours, she could see she was making inroads. Once her car was full to the roof with items, she drove to the local Red Cross charity shop and dropped off boxes for donation. Every few hours, she would return again to donate more items, each time greeted enthusiastically by the cheerful old lady who was working behind the counter. By the end of the day, she had managed to get through the majority of the boxes. The little old lady at the charity shop helped Tiffany organize a Red Cross truck to come and take away the bulky furniture the following day. By the end of the day, Tiffany had condensed the storage shed full of items down to six boxes of photo albums, jewellery and odd sentimental items. The job had been challenging but to finally finish was cathartic and Tiffany felt satisfied that she had managed to tick off the first task of her post-holiday to-do list.

Tiffany drove to her aunty and uncle's house. As they were still travelling, she had said that she would check in on the place every week and on days when she was seeking solitude, would even stay the night. She unloaded a box from the boot of her car that held some of her mum's items that she felt Aunty Jody would want and carried it up to her aunty's bedroom. Tiffany then ran a hot bath and sank down in it, letting the strain of the day wash away. When the water finally began to cool off, Tiffany got out and rugged herself up in her mum's fluffy pink robe. Tiffany was weary and as there was no fresh food in the house, she made herself some two-minute noodles (the unofficial diet of all university students) and sat in the lounge room watching trashy television.

Within an hour, the exhaustion of the day had caught up with her and she fell asleep on the luxuriously soft leather lounge; only stirring in the early hours of the morning to switch off the television, before dozing back off to sleep in the soft cocoon of her mum's robe.

The following day, Tiffany set herself the challenge to address the estate's financials. She had felt a storeroom full of boxes and furniture was daunting but the endless list of companies that sent bills regularly was confronting. Some bills were obvious, like council rates for the house, but the vast majority were from companies of whom she had never heard, and whose products and services were not known to her. Tiffany took the last financial year records and coded them. She highlighted companies whose bills could continue in green highlighter, companies whose products or services were no longer required in pink highlighter and left the rest blank. Over ten sheets of transactions, the majority of each page was untouched. Each bill left un-highlighted required her to research the company and whether she could discontinue their service.

The task was gruelling and time-consuming. Once Tiffany located a company that she no longer wanted to use, she had to track down their contact details, then call them to explain the cancellation so that she could send the correct notification to end the service. She set herself the task to get through ten companies a week. By breaking it down into small chunks, she felt better able to deal with the overwhelming research and paperwork.

After six weeks, Tiffany had to put this task aside to focus on the end of year assessments and exams. The dorm was eerily quiet as all the students bunkered down to study. Sarah knocked at Tiffany's door.

'Hey, Tiff, have you got a minute?'

'Yeah, come in. I could do with a break.'

'I'm freaking out,' Sarah confided, grimacing at her confession.

'Everyone freaks out at this time of year. Just think, this time in a fortnight, it will all be over and you will be back to partying.'

'No. I'm freaking out because my period is late. Like a week late.'

Tiffany gasped. She hadn't expected this revelation. 'Okay. Have you done a pregnancy test?' Tiffany asked.

'No. I'm too scared,' Sarah replied, her hands shaking nervously.

'Your period might be late from stress. You know, after my parents died, my system went haywire and I didn't have a period for several months. The doctor told me it is normal when you are under stress. Why don't we go to buy a test and then you can do it and find out if you are actually pregnant? You can't make a plan without knowing the facts.'

'I guess so. The problem is that if I am actually pregnant, I'm not even sure who the father is. I hooked up with Aaron a few weeks ago and then had a drunken romp with Caleb a few nights later. I'm so deep in shit.'

'Let's not jump ahead. Firstly, do the test and then you can go from there. I'll drive you to the pharmacy now if you like.'

'Thanks, Tiff, you're a lifesaver. I'm so nervous.

What if I am pregnant? I can't be a single mother and drop out of uni – my parents will kill me.'

Within half an hour, Sarah exited the ensuite in Tiffany's room with a plastic stick in hand. Tears streamed down her cheeks. 'It's fucking positive. I'm pregnant. What the hell am I supposed to do? I don't even know who the dad is.'

Tiffany wrapped her friend in a hug. 'Shhh. Everything will be okay. You have time to think things through. You can't be too far along. I think that for the next two weeks you have to focus on getting through your exams and then you can work out what you plan on doing.'

Sobs racked Sarah's body. 'I can't believe I'm such a fuck up. What the hell have I done?'

'Don't be so hard on yourself. You've been living life to the fullest but, unfortunately, it's come back to bite you. It's not the end of the world. You're not too young to have a child – plenty of people your age have kids. You would just have to put it in childcare while you work. Or if you don't want to keep it, there are plenty of people that would give their right arm to adopt your baby.'

'I can't have the baby and I certainly wouldn't want to give it to strangers to raise it. I just have to get an abortion. There's no other option,' Sarah sighed, deflated.

'Don't you have an ethical issue with killing

your child?' Tiffany asked.

'It's not really a child; it's just a collection of cells. I don't think I can wait until after my exams to do this. I will call and make an appointment as soon as possible. If need be, I will apply for misadventure to have my exam marks averaged from my assessments.'

'How have you done in your assessments this semester? I thought you worked on the premise that you would manage to scrape by with a pass if you aced your exam?'

'Shit. You're right. Oh well, if necessary, I will just have to take this semester's courses again. There's no way, even if I did sit the exams, that I can concentrate on studying with this hanging over my head.'

'It's a big decision. Don't you think that maybe you should sleep on it and give it time to sink in before you decide what to do?'

'There's nothing to consider. I'm not going to throw away my life because of this stupid mistake.' Sarah reached out and grabbed Tiffany's arm. 'Will you go with me? You're the only one that I've told about this.'

Tiffany was speechless. She did not agree with abortion on principle. Given how hard her parents had tried to have her, she fervently believed a baby's life was not something to terminate. 'Umm, I don't think I can,' she stammered, 'you know, with my exams and everything.'

Sarah's face blanched. 'Oh okay. Don't worry then,' she said coldly before stumbling out of Tiffany's room.

'Sarah,' Tiffany called out to her dorm mate's retreating back, but Sarah continued to walk with her head down, ignoring the pleas from her friend. Tiffany felt like she had let her friend down in her time of need, but at the same time, it was a sensitive issue and one where they clearly had different ethical beliefs.

Opening her textbook once more to resume studying, Tiffany stared blankly at the page, the words swum as tears pooled in her eyes. She wasn't even sure why she was so upset, whether it was guilt for not feeling able to help Sarah or the thought that Sarah would kill her own child when Tiffany knew better than anyone how precious life was.

CHAPTER 16

Tiffany had one last group assignment due for her communications subject before the end of semester. She was teamed up with another student, Charlie, and they had been given the task of determining the impact of social media on the psyche of teenagers. Luckily, Charlie had a friend who was a teacher at a local high-school who had volunteered a group of students to participate in a survey they had developed. Tiffany had spent weeks creating a questionnaire asking students if they used social media, how often, how many hours a day they were on it and how it made them feel.

Walking into the classroom, the smell of whiteboard markers and the sight of the desks lined up in rows reminded Tiffany of her schooling. So much had happened in Tiffany's life within the last year, it was hard to believe she had only completed school less than a year ago.

Tiffany's research group had decided to go against the grain of popular belief that social media was evil and had, instead, hypothesized that social media was not all bad and that the stigma of not being on social media had a greater impact on a teenager's social standing than the possible bullying associated with being on it. After extensive testing, Tiffany and Charlie theorized that kids who weren't on social media found the social isolation of not being part of conversations and current trends was worse for their self-esteem than those feeling depressed by comparing themselves to unrealistic portrayals of other's lives on social media. They also found that levels of bullying didn't show a great variation from those using social media or not.

Tiffany was excited to write up the final findings and present them to her cohort. She was sure that their findings would be controversial, but that gave her even more motivation to do a thorough job of analysing the surveys. Tiffany threw herself wholeheartedly into her university assignments, as it was the only thing in her life that she really had any control over. As she and Charlie tidied up the classroom they had been using, a man with a folder leaned against the wall in the hallway, patiently waiting to access the room. He was obviously a teacher wanting to prepare for his next class. As they left the room, Charlie turned and thanked the man for his patience. Tiffany smiled in his direction to show her gratitude. When she realised that she recognised the man as Harley Jefferson, her smile dropped. Her heart began to race and her blood boiled. She would never come to terms with the fact that he had been spared a jail sentence. She had a vague recollection that he had been training as a teacher. It was one of the reasons the defence had painted him as a saint, but she was sure he couldn't be qualified yet. She wondered whether he was some perverted paedophile loitering in the hallway of a school, waiting for his next victim.

Not wanting to dwell on his presence, Tiffany clenched her teeth and scowled as she briskly walked away, shaking her head.

Charlie caught up with Tiffany. 'Are you okay?'

Tiffany nodded. 'I'm fine.'

'Do you want to go back to the library to pull this all together?'

Tiffany didn't feel like spending time in anyone's company. 'I'm happy to collate the results and then we can meet next week to finalise our speech.'

Charlie shrugged his shoulders. 'If you're okay with that, then that would be great. I've really got to study. My first exam is next week.'

'Yeah, mine too. I can't wait for all the assessments and exams to be over.'

'I know right.' Charlie handed over the surveys to Tiffany. 'Well, just let me know when you are ready to go over the results. Thanks for everything, Tiff.'

'No problems.' Tiffany replied. She gave him a

tight smile, still wound up by her encounter with Harley Jefferson.

The last day of exams. The last day of the year. The last big celebration for 2016. Tiffany had made a promise to herself after her Fijian holiday to try to live life to the fullest, which included socialising more. Completing a year's studies, particularly given the emotional rollercoaster she had been on throughout the year, was the perfect excuse to let her hair down, relax and have fun.

The college had taken on a carnival type atmosphere and it was hard to not get swept up in the hype. All the students were on a mission to party. Tiffany danced with a group of friends, all of them periodically gulping down the contents of a home-made alcoholic punch from red plastic tumblers.

Tiffany spotted Sarah walking towards the dance floor. As they made eye-contact, Sarah glanced away and turned to walk in the opposite direction.

Tiffany strode after her, 'Sarah, how are you?'

'Like you care,' Sarah said, flicking her long dark curls over her shoulder.

'I really do care about you, Sarah,' Tiffany said, hurt that her friend was being so cold. 'What did you decide to do?'

'It's really none of your business and something I definitely don't want to discuss here.'

'Fair enough. I just want you to know that I'm here if you need to talk.' Tiffany reached out and gave Sarah's shoulder a squeeze.

'I'm all good,' Sarah said, plastering a fake smile on her face before skulking away. Tiffany's hand dropped by her side. The joy of the evening had suddenly dissipated after she had been left spurned by the awkward encounter.

Sunani came and wrapped her arm around Tiffany's shoulders. 'What was that about? I don't know what Sarah's problem is lately but she has issues. She is so self-absorbed.'

'I think she's been feeling a bit stressed lately,' Tiffany responded vaguely.

'I think we have all been feeling a bit stressed, and now it's time to de-stress and party.' Sunani clinked her plastic cup against Tiffany's cup, 'Cheers!'

'Cheers.' Tiffany smiled and drank the strong syrupy liquor.

Aaron approached the girls, inserting himself between them as he wrapped his arms around their shoulders. 'Are you girls coming to the pub?' he asked.

Sunani smiled widely, 'Yep, let's get going.'

As they were walking towards the pub, Aaron turned his attention to Tiffany. 'You're looking hot tonight, Tiff. You know when you first started here you looked like a bored stiff corpse, but you've really come into your own now. If you want to become friends with benefits with me, just say the word.' Aaron winked cheekily at Tiffany, making her skin crawl.

Tiffany shrugged Aaron's arm from her shoulder, 'Thanks, but no thanks.'

Aaron looked crestfallen, 'Why?'

'Firstly, I don't have casual flings. Secondly, I don't date my friend's exes and, finally, I don't date douchebags.'

'Ouch! Tell me how you really feel,' Aaron said sarcastically, clearly taken aback from what Tiffany assumed was an unfamiliar feeling of rejection.

'Seriously, Aaron, you just told me I looked like a corpse at the start of the year, at the time when I had just buried my parents. That was so callous.'

Aaron had the grace to blush. 'Sorry, Tiff, I wasn't thinking. I was trying to give you a compliment to say you look hot now.'

'Aaron, you're just not my type. The brunette over there has been watching you intently while we've been talking. Maybe you should go introduce yourself.'

Aaron cast his gaze in the direction of the girl. 'Okay, I think I will.' Like a small child distracted from a tantrum with a new shiny toy, Aaron turned away from Tiffany and Sunani to focus his energy on the mystery brunette.

Sunani turned to Tiffany, 'I can't believe you turned down Aaron. I don't think anyone has ever done that before.'

'He has an overinflated ego. Honestly, I would rather go through life alone than be in a relationship with someone like him. There's a reason he is known as a male slut!'

'But think what cute babies you two could make' Sunani said giggling.

'I can get donor sperm and have a cute baby without all the hassle of having to deal with such a jerk. Honestly, he should be with Sarah consoling her, not here chatting me up.'

'Why does Sarah need consoling?' Sunani asked; her interest piqued.

'Oh, I don't know. She has just been stressed,' Tiffany said vaguely, trying to cover up her slip of discretion. 'Maybe it's because she is heartbroken from having a fling with Aaron?'

'Or maybe she is having problems dividing her time between Aaron and Caleb. I saw her snuggled up with Caleb a few weeks ago,' Sunani said gossiping.

'I don't know. Let's not talk about Sarah anymore, let's go get our groove on,' Tiffany said, leading the way inside the pub towards the dance floor.

CHAPTER 17

The college dorm was unusually quiet. With the majority of boarders having gone home for the summer break, only those without a home to return to were left. Tiffany reclined on her bed; binge-watching a show on Netflix to distract her from her looming birthday and the subsequent anniversary of her parents' death.

Gabby was returning from Bathurst and was keen to party, but Tiffany felt it disrespectful to party at a time when it marked the first anniversary since she had lost her parents.

The morning of her nineteenth birthday, Tiffany awoke to knocking on her door.

'Happy birthday, Sunshine,' Gabby said, smiling while balancing gifts and a box in her arms.

Tiffany smiled. 'Thanks, Gab. Come in.'

Tiffany caught sight of her reflection in the mirror. Her hair was tousled and her eyes were squinting, still trying to adjust to being awake. She would die if anyone saw her like this, but Gabby didn't count as she was like a sister. In contrast,

Gabby was fresh-faced, her makeup making her look like she was glowing.

'I've missed you so much,' Gabby said, hugging Tiffany whilst rocking her side to side.

'I've missed you too.' Tiffany held Gabby at arm's length, 'you look different. It's not your hair, what has changed?'

'I've had my lips done. Do you like my fuller pout?' Gabby asked, puckering her lips to exaggerate the effect.

'It looks great. Very sexy.'

'Enough about me – you're the birthday girl. Here, open this,' Gabby said thrusting an ornately decorated gift into her hands.

Tiffany took her time opening the present, trying not to destroy the packaging. Inside was a gorgeous dress and an exquisite necklace with matching earrings.

'They are beautiful, thank you so much, Gab,' Tiffany said, hugging her friend once more.

'My pleasure, Treasure. Now, for my real pleasure, I brought us Nutella doughnuts for breakfast.'

Gabby opened the white cardboard pastry box with flare displaying the white glazed plump balls of dough. Tiffany's mouth began to water as she looked at the sugary treats. 'Yum. You are truly the best friend a girl could ask for!'

'I know you don't really want to celebrate today,

but I figure these don't count as a celebration, just a naughty treat.'

'I agree,' Tiffany said, grabbing a doughnut and taking a bite that left Nutella oozing out of the centre. With a mouth full of food, Tiffany looked at Gabby, 'These are delicious. You have to have one.'

'With pleasure,' Gabby said, sinking her teeth into the decadent treat.

The girls spent the day sunbaking on the beach and then Gabby suggested they both visit a tattoo parlour to each get a new tattoo. For a long time, Tiffany had wanted to get her parents' dates of birth tattooed on her ribs and being so close to the anniversary of their death, it seemed like an appropriate way to honour them.

'What are you getting?' Tiffany asked Gabby.

'I thought I'd get a diamond tattooed on my hip.'

'Why a diamond?' Tiffany queried.

'Because diamonds are a girl's best friend,' Gabby replied. 'Plus, I want guys to know that I love diamonds and that they should penny up to buy me lots of them.'

Tiffany laughed. 'You crack me up, Gab.'

Tiffany had been prepared for the sensation of the needle piercing her skin, but her ribs were way more sensitive than the fleshier areas she had previously tattooed. After twenty minutes, Tiffany looked at the end result and was thrilled with how perfect it looked.

When Gabby lay on the table, she began to hyperventilate. 'Hold my hand, Tiff.'

Tiffany held her best friend's hand tightly. 'You will be fine, Gab.'

Gabby gripped Tiffany's hand so tightly that the bones in her fingers crunched together. Tiffany was pretty sure getting the tattoo on her ribs was less painful than holding Gabby's hand.

When the ordeal was over, Gabby admired her new tattoo. 'I love it. Doesn't it look sophisticated?'

Tiffany nodded. She wondered whether Gabby would regret that tattoo in years to come. Tiffany felt confident that as her tattoos held significance, she would love them until the day she died.

That evening, they went to dinner at a cheap and cheerful Italian restaurant in Manly.

'Thanks for such a great day. I'm so glad I was able to keep it low key. Mind you, apart from you, my BFF, there's not really anyone around to celebrate with.'

'I could have rustled up friends to celebrate but I know it is a hard time for you. What have you got planned for tomorrow?' Gabby asked tenderly.

'I'm going to visit the cemetery and then I'm going to go to North Head and throw some roses into the water of Sydney Harbour. Mum and Dad loved sailing and I think that would be a nice memorial for them.'

'Would you like me to come?' Gab asked.

'No thanks. I think I will just do it on my own, but thanks for offering.'

'Well, I will be around if you change your mind. Do you want to come back to my parents' place tonight? We can watch a movie. You're welcome to stay if you like.'

'Thanks, Gab, but I think I will just stay at mine. It would be weird to wake up in your house as I did the same time last year.'

'Of course. I hadn't even thought of that. Sorry, Tiff.'

'It's not a problem.'

'Tiff, I just wanted to say how proud I am of how well you have coped this year. It has been rough and I know I wouldn't have dealt with it as well as you have. It's so weird to think this time last year we were dancing up a storm at your eighteenth birthday party. That was such a cool party.'

Tiffany smiled, 'Yeah, it was, wasn't it? It's just hard to think about the good times that night without my memories being clouded by the tragedy that occurred later on. I often think that if I hadn't had a party then Mum and Dad wouldn't have been driving home and been killed.'

'Hun, you can't feel guilty about having a party and fun. Your parents were having a great time that night, as was everyone there. It wasn't your party that killed them, it was an out of control driver.'

'I know, but if I could wind back the clock, I wouldn't have had a party. I'd do anything to still have my parents alive.'

'I know, I miss them too,' Gabby said, tears pooling in her eyes. 'They were like second parents to me.'

Tiffany swiped at her eyes angrily, 'Let's change the subject. I've spent too much of this year crying. My resolution for the next year of my life is to smile more and cry less.'

Gabby raised her glass, 'Cheers to that.'

The following morning, Tiffany arose to a clear, bright, sunny day. As she lay in bed, she tried to dissect her feelings about it being the anniversary of her parents' deaths. Part of her welcomed the anniversary; a turning point in her grief. She had successfully survived a year on her own. The greater part of her felt alone, abandoned and desperately sad that she would never see her parents again. She had spent the last few months trying to mask her grief and contain her emotions, but for once, she let down her guard and openly wept. The events of a year ago rushed back like a home movie in her mind. The gut instinct when she saw all the missed calls from her aunty, to the confirmation of her worst suspicions, to visiting the morgue to hug the lifeless bodies of her parents. Every memory was as clear as if it happened yesterday.

Tiffany showered, rinsing away her tears. As she dressed, she decided it was not a day for makeup.

Her first stop was at a florist to buy two bouquets for her parents' matching graves and two single white roses. As she walked towards their headstones, she could see fresh flowers laid at their graves. Harley Jefferson had obviously visited and the thought left her simultaneously irate and grateful. She didn't want people to forget her parents just because they weren't physically around anymore, but it seemed wrong that the person most attentive to their graves was their killer. Whilst she could never imagine a day that she could forgive him for his actions that night, she could see that he was genuinely remorseful. Her feelings towards him confused her. She wanted to hate him and to get revenge, but at the same time felt his respect for her parents maybe deemed him worthy of forgiveness. Rather than dwell on him, Tiffany focused her thoughts on her parents.

In whispered tones, she talked to her parents; thanking them for being amazing, attentive and loving parents. She also talked of how much she missed them and the loneliness brought about by their absence. She talked and cried, then talked some more until there were no more words to say. A white butterfly flew around Tiffany's head before it landed lightly on her bouquet by her mother's headstone. Tiffany took it as a sign from beyond the grave; a reassurance she had been heard and that her parents' spirits were surrounding her.

Tiffany left the cemetery and then drove to North Head. Standing upon the cliff top, the salty brine mist was lifted on the strong nor-easterly breeze. After a few words uttered, Tiffany kissed each rose and threw them off the cliffs into the bubbling sea below. The small white rose heads bobbed above the water, dancing together in a specially choreographed dance of love. In that moment, Tiffany was grateful that her parents had died together. Their love was a bond that had seen them through heartache and triumph; strengthened by the addition of their miracle child and then finally melded as together they took their final breaths.

By the end of the day, Tiffany was emotionally spent but the ritual of visiting her parents' graves and her own personal memorial had left her feeling lighter as she shed the grief that had weighed heavily on her for the last year. She knew her love for her parents would never dim, but at the same time, she was confident that with each passing day, she would grow stronger and cope better with their loss.

CHAPTER 18

Back in the comfort of her dorm room, Tiffany had assumed her favourite position, lying flat on her bed, her eyes glued to Netflix. Her mobile phone rang next to her ear, startling her at a suspenseful time in the show.

'Hello,' Tiffany answered.

'Hi, Babe,' Gabby replied, her bubbly voice an injection of warmth and comfort.

'Gab, how are you?'

'I'm awesome. I've got the most exciting news. My parents have just told me we are going to Europe for a white Christmas. We leave next week. I can't believe it,' Gabby squealed with excitement.

'Wow. That's awesome,' Tiffany responded, trying to garner some sense of excitement for her. In the back of her mind, she was thinking about how much she would miss her best friend over the Christmas break. She had hoped with Gabby home from university in Bathurst, the two of them would wile away the days sunbaking on the beach or shopping in malls.

'Can you come over? I want to work out my wardrobe. I'm not sure that I have clothes that will be warm enough. We are heading to Lucerne in Switzerland for Christmas, then Paris for New Year's.'

'You're such a high flyer. Do your parents want to adopt me?' Tiffany said in jest.

'Oh, Tiff, I'm so sorry. I wasn't thinking about you being alone at Christmas. I can ask them if you can join us.'

'No, don't be silly. I was just joking. I don't want to join your family on their holiday. I'm just planning on having a relaxing time here. Enjoying time without university assignments. I've also got a heap of stuff to do for my trust. Plus, you know me, I love the warmth of summer. I wouldn't want to give it up to be in the snow.'

'Okay, fair enough. So, are you free to come over now?'

'Sure, Babe. I'll see you soon.'

Driving to Gabby's parents' house, Tiffany tried to buoy her spirits so that she didn't dampen Gabby's excitement. Tiffany realised she needed to get used to being alone and didn't want people to pity her. She knew Aunty Jody and Uncle Alex were spending Christmas in the Greek Isles, but there was a possibility she could celebrate with her cousins, Josh and Jack. She made a mental note to call them to see if they had plans.

As Tiffany pulled up in the driveway of Gabby's house, she had a sudden flashback of standing on the concrete driveway when Aunty Jody had told her of her parents' deaths. She hadn't expected to be confronted with the sharp, painful memory and she broke out in a sweat as tears threatened to pool in her eyes.

Gabby opened the front door of the house and ran towards the car. Taking a deep breath to calm herself, Tiffany plastered a smile on her face to mask her pain and opened the car door, throwing herself into Gabby's outstretched arms.

'I'm going to Europe, I'm going to Europe,' Gabby sang like a toddler.

'Those Swiss boys better watch out,' Tiffany teased.

Gabby laughed and wrapped an arm around Tiffany's shoulders. 'Come inside, my parents are keen to see you. They haven't seen you in ages. But make sure you don't get stuck talking to them; I need your advice on what to pack for Europe. I can't believe this time next week I will be on a plane to the other side of the world. I'm so friggin' excited.' Gabby's face beamed and Tiffany felt herself become swept up in her best friend's elation.

After hours of pulling out every item of clothing in Gabby's wardrobe, the girls had tentatively packed what items were appropriate for the cold winter climate in Europe and had made a long list of items to purchase.

They then dedicated their time to searching the internet for the right items of clothing, knowing that the local shops would only stock Summer clothes so close to Christmas. Being the opposite season, the girls were thrilled to locate some great bargain items, which were perfectly suited for Gabby's holiday.

Every day for a week, the girls were inseparable. Tiffany wanted to soak up being in Gabby's company so that once her best friend was overseas, she could reflect on the fun times they had spent together. The days flashed past in a blur of activities. Each of the girls aware that their time together was precious, particularly as their university choices had meant they had been deprived of hanging out much throughout the year.

The evening before Gabby's trip, Tiffany logged onto her university email account to get the results of her exams and assessments. Tiffany was thrilled that her hard work and effort was paying off. She got two distinctions and four high-distinctions. She shared her news with Gabby, who had a credit point average.

'Oh, Tiff, your parents would be so proud. You always were a high achiever. I'm just planning on coasting through. I figure there is no need to put yourself under too much pressure because that's what will happen when you get a real job. At the end of the day, as long as I end up with a degree with my name on it, I'll be happy.'

Tiffany laughed, 'We really are chalk and cheese.'

'Yep, we're yin and yang,' Gabby replied, holding her dark hair up against Tiffany's blonde locks. 'We complement each other perfectly.'

The morning of Gabby's overseas trip, Tiffany drove Gabby's family to the airport. Gabby was a ball of nervous excitement and Tiffany was torn between not wanting her friend to go for her own selfish reasons and being thrilled that Gabby would have an experience of a lifetime. Gabby's parents were keen to go through security to ensure they were on time for when their flight was called for boarding. Tiffany and Gabby embraced.

'Have an amazing time. I want all the juicy details about those French and Swiss men when you return.'

'I'll keep a diary just so I can keep up with all the admirers,' Gabby said facetiously while batting her eyelids and pouting her new fuller lips.

'I'll miss you so much,' Tiffany said, giving Gabby one last hug.

'I'll miss you more,' Gabby said, hugging her

friend tighter.

Eventually, Gabby's family walked behind the 'Departures' sign and disappeared from sight, leaving Tiffany with an acute feeling of loneliness.

CHAPTER 19

Christmas had always been a time for a casual family get together with Aunty Jody, Uncle Alex, Jack and Josh, relaxing by the pool, eating seafood and salad. A day of indulgence with the house full of love, presents and a ridiculous amount of sugary snacks. The highlight had always been a Secret Santa where crazy or offensive (sometimes both) presents were traded. The more ludicrous the gift, the better. The laughs were infectious.

Christmas celebrations this year could not have been more opposite. After calling her cousins to make plans, Tiffany had discovered Josh was going on a surfari up the north coast of Australia and planned on freshly caught fish baked in foil on an open fire as his lunchtime feast. Jack had planned to celebrate with his girlfriend's family and half-heartedly invited Tiffany to join them, but it seemed like too much of an intrusion.

Tiffany's grandparents on her Dad's side had formally invited her to join them for Christmas lunch. Although, of course, she loved her grandparents, she had never been close to them and didn't feel very relaxed in their presence. Lunch was prepared by her Grandma, a traditional cooked ham, turkey and baked vegetables; showing no regard for the fact that being the middle of summer, the temperature was close to thirty-five degrees Celsius.

Upon arriving at her Grandparent's home, Tiffany was warmly greeted and ushered into the formal lounge room for a glass of punch. They exchanged gifts, each handing over impersonal presents of candles and gift vouchers, the type of gifts that scream that you don't know one another's tastes and interests. After the obligatory crooning over how much they each loved their presents, Tiffany was escorted to the dining room for lunch.

The table was formally decorated and Tiffany and her grandparents each took a turn at pulling a Christmas cracker that encased a cheap plastic trinket, an atrocious joke and a limp brightly coloured paper hat, that they all put on their heads in mock joviality. Tiffany's grandparents quizzed her on university, the conversation more like an interview than a heartfelt chat.

Although she was already acutely aware of missing her parents, the stuffiness of her surroundings, so polar opposite to the Christmas' she knew and loved, made her feel even more bereft at being alone.

After a bowl of Christmas pudding that she knew

her Grandma would have spent days making, Tiffany felt uncomfortably full and tired. She longed to escape, but out of politeness, she offered to clean up the kitchen. To her great dismay, her grandparents agreed and she spent the next hour entrenched in the kitchen, washing up the dishes as her grandparents napped in their recliner chairs in the lounge room. Their light snores muffled by a Christmas movie playing quietly in the background.

Once finished with her chores, Tiffany made a pot of tea and carried it to the lounge room on a silver tray. She hoped the noise of the rattling china cups and clanging cutlery would be sufficient to wake her grandparents from their slumber.

After three and a half hours, Tiffany felt it was finally acceptable to leave. She appreciated the fact that her grandparents had invited her to spend Christmas with them so she wasn't alone, but she made a mental note for the next year to make other plans in advance.

'Thank you so much for the gifts and the lovely lunch,' Tiffany said, kissing her Grandma's cheek.

'You are always welcome here, Tiffany,' her Grandfather said, patting her cheek roughly.

'Thanks, Grandpa,' Tiffany said, relieved to finally be leaving. 'Goodbye,' she said, waving as she made a hasty retreat to her car.

CHAPTER 20

With Gabby overseas and most of her friends gone, Tiffany decided it was time to finalise sorting out her trust fund. She located another unknown supplier 'Gibson Incorporated' and tracked down an invoice for $800 for twelve month's storage. Tiffany wondered what her parents had stored. She had thought that all their possessions had been put into storage in the unit she had cleared out months before.

Tiffany rang the phone number on the invoice. 'Good morning, Gibson's clinic.'

'Umm, hi. I just wanted to ask what storage you offer?'

'If you go to our website, you will see our fees for storage. It starts at $252 for sperm and goes up from there for eggs and embryos.'

Tiffany suddenly understood why these items had not been included in the storage unit. 'My parents died last year and I have inherited their estate. I have been paying for annual storage. Is there someone there who can clarify what my parents have stored?'

'I can put you through to our accounts department and they can assist you. One moment.'

Tiffany's mind reeled. She had always known that she was conceived through IVF but had never realised her parents had spare embryos. She would have desperately loved a sibling and it would have meant she wouldn't have been left all alone when her parents died.

'Accounts, how may I help?'

'I'm enquiring about invoice number 160354 that was paid last year for 12 month's storage. The invoice doesn't detail what is being stored. Are you able to clarify this for me?'

Tiffany listened to the rapid tapping of a keyboard. 'Yes, it is the storage of one frozen embryo from 1996.'

'Thank you,' Tiffany responded, her mind reeling with the revelation that this embryo could have been her twin.

'Can I help with anything else?'

'Not at the moment. Thanks for your help.' Tiffany put her phone down. Obviously, her parents had tried so hard to conceive and had never been able to bring themselves to terminate the embryo nor donate it to another couple.

Tiffany was in shock. The fact that she was now left with the task of killing her unborn sibling was too difficult a concept to contemplate. After already losing her parents, there was no way she could be responsible for another death in the family.

Considering other options, Tiffany was certain she didn't want her sibling growing up in a stranger's family.

A knock at the door roused Tiffany out of her state of contemplation.

Opening the door, she was surprised to see Aunty Jody standing on the other side. 'Surprise,' Jody said, throwing her arms out wide.

Tiffany squealed with delight and hugged her aunty tight. 'What are you doing here? You weren't due back for a few weeks.'

'I know, but we got homesick. We flew in last night. I asked the boys to keep it a secret so I could surprise you.'

'I'm so glad you're back. I missed you guys. I'd offer for you to come in but there's really only my bed to sit on. I'll just grab my stuff and we can head down to the café and you can fill me in on your trip. Your photos on Facebook looked like you were having a ball.'

'It was great, but travelling makes you really appreciate what you have at home. I thought going on our dream trip would make us forget the pain of the last year, but I must admit, I wanted to be able to share the places we went and the things we did with your mum. It actually made me miss her all the more. Plus, I missed the boys and you, so in the end, we decided to cut the trip short and come back to our loved ones.'

'There's no place like home,' Tiffany said, whilst in her mind thinking about the fact that she felt like she no longer had a place she could call home. Her dorm room was a place to sleep and study and it served its purpose, but it had none of the warmth or affection of a home.

After hearing the funny anecdotes from her aunty's time overseas, the conversation turned to Tiffany and how she was coping.

'I'm good, thanks, although I found out something today that has left me in a quandary of what to do. Mum and Dad had a frozen embryo that they have had in storage for the last twenty years. I can't bring myself to destroy it, but I can't keep paying to have it stored indefinitely.'

'I assumed your parents must have destroyed that years ago. I wonder whether they kept it as a type of insurance policy in case something ever happened to you?'

'That's a bit macabre. Maybe they secretly wanted to have another child but just didn't get around to it.'

'Have you considered donating it to someone who is infertile?'

'No. I couldn't stand the thought of this child, who in effect is my twin, growing up in a stranger's family. If Mum and Dad had wanted that, then they would have donated it years ago.'

'So, what other option is there? You could donate it to science.'

'The last thing I want is for the embryo to be chopped up in a lab. This embryo is the only genetic link to immediate family that I have left.'

'Well, you could always give birth to it and it would be your 'saughter', you know, sister/daughter and it would make you her 'mister', you know, mother/sister,' Jody said, chuckling at her joke.

'Can you imagine?' Tiffany laughed and rolled her eyes.

'What are you thinking you will do?'

'I don't know. I guess for the moment I will just keep paying for storage until I work out what to do.'

After spending the morning with her aunty, Tiffany lay on her bed, automatically turning on Netflix out of habit. Lying there, she struggled to focus on the show and in annoyance switched off her computer. She decided to go to the beach for a walk. People would begin to think she was a vampire given how pale her skin was in the middle of summer.

Tiffany took a deep breath of the salty mist, her feet burrowed into the warm sand and she relaxed with the soothing sound of the crashing waves. Watching kids frolicking on the shore, Tiffany started to walk along the shoreline, weaving up and down the sand in sync with the ebb and flow of the waves. She felt calm, surrounded by crowds of people, yet alone, able to focus on the jumbled thoughts in her mind that were swirling like an eddy on the water.

Her conversation with her aunty regarding the frozen embryo played on her mind. She had playfully joked about Tiffany giving birth to the baby, which at the time had seemed an absurd idea, but as Tiffany was definite about not wanting to pursue the other options available to her, the idea of her giving birth to the child became less and less preposterous. She hadn't thought she was at a time in her life when she would want to settle down with a child, but hadn't she only recently told Sarah that she wasn't too young to have a baby? Tiffany was lonely and sorely missed having any family. Maybe the only logical solution was to have the baby. She had inherited enough money to cover their living expenses and she could still continue to study at university and then start work when the child started school. A sudden maternal feeling welled up inside her. Tiffany couldn't kill her sibling and she couldn't give it away, but she could protect it and give her sibling life, which might, in turn, give her a new reason to live.

A feeling of excitement rose in her chest, the first fluttering of a new direction in life. Tiffany watched a mother holding the hands of her toddler as she jumped her over the waves rolling up the shore. Peals of laughter floated up from the little girl and Tiffany could suddenly picture herself in the shoes of the mother. She felt protective over the unborn child and wanted to do all she could to make sure the baby would be safe, loved and able to reach its potential.

Finding a deserted patch of beach, Tiffany sat down and reached for her phone. She called Gabby, hoping that the time zone in Europe was compatible.

'Hello?' a groggy voice answered the phone.

'Gab, it's me,' Tiffany said excitedly.

Gabby stifled a yawn, 'Hey there, what's up?'

'I'm thinking of having a baby,' Tiffany blurted out.

'What the? What are you talking about?'

'I've just found out that Mum and Dad had a frozen embryo they never used and rather than kill it or give it away, I thought I should have the baby.'

'Sorry, Tiff, my brain isn't working properly coz you just woke me up. Did you just say you want to give birth to a frozen embryo that is your parents? Is that incest? I don't know what it is, but it is all sorts of wrong.'

'Not really. Just think about it for a minute. I could give this child life and it would give me family again. I know I can't bring my parents back, but I can bring to life their offspring; my sibling.'

'Tiff, this is the time of your life where you should be concentrating on getting a boyfriend, travelling, partying, finishing uni and getting a job. Don't you realise having a baby now will jeopardize all those things?'

'I get it, but you know family is more important to me than all those things. This would be the greatest parting gift I could give my parents. Mum gave up trying to have babies because she struggled with infertility. There's a chance I could bring my parents' dream to life. Even more importantly, I will have a family again; a second chance of belonging. I don't have to be alone anymore, which would mean the world to me.'

'Girl, you're crazy! Just promise me you will think long and hard about this. You know whatever you decide, I will support you.'

'Thanks,' Tiffany said, her voice softening, 'you are the one person in the world that is always there for me. I mean, not physically – you're on the other side of the world at the moment, but emotionally, you're always there for me.'

'If I had known you were considering having a baby soon, I would have dragged you on this trip with my family so you could see Europe before you focus on changing nappies. Paris is c'est magnifique,' Gabby said in a corny French accent. 'Everywhere you look is a famous icon. The sun is only just rising and looking out my window, through the mist, I can see the Eiffel Tower. It looks like a postcard, or a scene from a romantic movie. Mum and I are going to the Louvre today to check out the Mona Lisa. It's so surreal!'

'It sounds awesome and I'm so glad you are having an amazing time. I have my whole life to travel, so I'm sure one day I will make it to Paris. You know they say home is where the heart is, and so, at the moment, the most important thing for me is to make a home, with a family, to help heal my heart.'

'N'aww. Can I be called Aunty Gabby?'

Tiffany laughed, 'Absolutely. As long as you promise to babysit all the time.'

'If your sibling is as cool as you are, then I will want to just hang around anyway!'

'I miss you, Gab. How long until you are due to come home?'

'Two more weeks of drinking French champagne and eating croissants and then I'll be back home.'

'When does your uni go back?'

'Not until the start of March, so I promise I'll hang out with you as much as I can when we get home.'

'Okay. I can't wait. All right, well I had better go. Enjoy the Louvre today.'

'Au revoir,' Gabby said once more in her tacky French accent before ending the phone call.

CHAPTER 21

Sitting in the stuffy reception area of the clinic, Tiffany's legs jiggled nervously as she awaited her name to be called. The beige plastic chairs were uncomfortable, the room bland and non-assuming. In search of a form of distraction, Tiffany grabbed a dog-eared magazine that was twelve months out of date. She flicked through it while simultaneously looking around the room at the other women awaiting their appointments. Most looked to be in their late thirties or early forties, some accompanied by men, some with supportive friends and a few, like her, sitting alone.

A gentleman with grey hair and glasses perched on the end of his nose, appeared in a doorway and after examining a cream manila folder, called out her name. Tiffany smiled and gave a small wave to indicate she was present. He nodded and with a stony face, ushered her into his room.

'You seem very young to need our services. How may I help you?' Dr Gibson said, staring at her, his pen poised above a blank page.

'Well, um, I am an IVF baby,' Tiffany said smiling, building up the courage to discuss her plans.

'Right,' Dr Gibson said, nodding as he scribbled a note.

'My parents had several rounds of IVF in 1996 and were only successful in giving birth to me. Both my parents died in a car crash at the end of 2015. Your clinic has been storing a frozen embryo of theirs for the last twenty years and I wanted to see what was involved in getting that embryo implanted in me.'

Taking a moment to gather his thoughts while he scribbled further notes in the file, Dr Gibson finally set his pen down. 'I'm sorry to hear about your parents' deaths. There is little chance that the embryo would still be viable and if it was, I'm afraid that it is unlikely our ethics committee would agree to this. Our admin staff can help you in arranging to humanely destroy the embryo or donate it to another couple.'

Tiffany was taken aback by his frosty demeanour. 'Can I just talk to you hypothetically for a moment? *If* I wanted to have this embryo implanted and *if* the ethics committee agreed, what steps would need to be taken?'

'Dear,' Dr Gibson said patronizingly, 'I can assure you the ethics committee *won't* agree as I am the head of the said committee, but *if* they did agree, you would need to have tests to check on your fertility and to determine the best time of month for implantation. The embryo would be taken out of storage and then tested to see if it was still viable. If it were deemed viable, it would be implanted. There is statistically only about a 20% chance it would take. Can I ask whether you have express written permission from your parents to have their embryo implanted?'

Tiffany shook her head slowly, feeling like a scolded child.

'Well, then it is clear that this won't be proceeding. You can see the receptionist on your way out to discuss your options going forward.'

'There's just one thing, Dr Gibson. I inherited that embryo; I own it. My parents may not have given me express permission to give birth to this child but neither did they give me permission to kill or donate it to someone else, yet you are saying I can do either of those. I'm confused as to why I can give it to someone else to use, but you won't let me use it myself? I'd like to request to present my case to your ethics committee to discuss my options.'

The doctor's brow furrowed, obviously not used to being confronted by a young woman. 'As you wish, however, I would suggest you don't get your hopes up as this is a very odd request and one that I am certain will not be granted.'

'Great,' Tiffany said with mock cheerfulness,

'just let me know when I can meet with the committee. You have a great day.'

Shaking his head ever so slightly, the doctor huffed as he scribbled further notes in the file. 'I'll be in touch.'

Keeping her head high and a fake smile plastered on her face, Tiffany paid the bill and then rushed to her car, breaking down in tears as soon as she was in the privacy of her car. She had never felt so humiliated and patronized in her life.

Once her emotions had calmed down, her anger grew. She was not going to take this negativity as a sign to stop, rather just as a hurdle on her way to regaining her family. Tiffany picked up the phone and called her Uncle Alex.

'Hi, Uncle Alex, it's Tiffany. How are you?'

Alex sounded genuinely happy to hear from her. 'Hi, Tiff. I'm great now that the jetlag has worn off. I'm just getting back into the swing of things. How are you?'

'I'm good thanks. Aunty Jody said you had a lovely trip, but I must admit it is nice to know you are both back home safe and sound.'

'Thanks, Tiff. What have you been up to?'

'Well,' Tiffany said hesitantly, trying to gain the courage to discuss her plans, 'I have been making enquiries about having a frozen embryo of Mum and Dad's implanted in me.'

'What?' Alex said with clear surprise upon

hearing Tiffany's intention.

'The problem is, the old codger of a doctor that I saw at the clinic that's storing the embryo said he had an ethical problem with it and shut me down. I have asked to meet with the ethics committee of the clinic, of which he is the head, for them to give me a formal determination. I just wanted to ask your advice, as you're a lawyer. What are my rights?'

'Hmm, that is an interesting question. I will have to do some research and get back to you.'

'That would be great. I assume after Mum and Dad died, you must have contacted the clinic to change the invoices to be paid by the trust fund. The clinic did that without question and I have been paying for the storage of the embryo. Wouldn't all of those things prove that I am the owner of the embryo; therefore, it is my choice what I do with it? The doctor said I can destroy it or I can donate it, so if I can do that, then why can't I have it implanted?'

'They are valid points, Tiff. I will look into it. Just an aside, have you given this much thought? I know you miss your parents, but is having a baby the best thing for you at this stage of life?'

'Uncle Alex, I know everyone will think I am nuts but the most important thing in the world for me is my family. If Mum hadn't had such problems with getting pregnant, she would have had this child. It's my chance to make that a reality, after all, they never decided to destroy the embryo, so maybe part of them always thought perhaps they would have the baby one day.'

'When is the committee meeting?'

'They haven't set a date, but I want to be prepared in advance,' Tiffany said stubbornly.

'Okay, I will make some enquiries and get back to you.'

'Thanks, Uncle Alex. I knew I could count on you.'

Alex knocked on the office door of Phil, a senior partner in his firm who was responsible for family law matters.

'Can I pick your brains for a minute?' Alex asked, entering Phil's office.

'Sure, take a seat.'

'My niece would like to know her rights regarding a frozen embryo she inherited when her parents died. She would like to have it implanted, but the clinic holding the embryo feels it is unethical. Do you know any cases that set a precedence in frozen embryos?'

'Were there any express instructions left in the will of what should happen with the embryo in the case of their death?'

'No. They just had a standard will, where they agreed that all their property would be divided equally between any surviving children. My niece was an only child. My sister-in-law and brother-in-law froze this embryo 20 years ago. I don't think back then either of them gave thought to what they would do if they died prematurely. I assume they were more focused on the health and wellbeing of the baby they did have through IVF.'

'Assisted reproduction is a bit of a grey area. The question is whether frozen embryos are considered property or people? Most cases I know of are either where a couple have divorced and one of the biological parents wants the right to use the embryos of their own accord, or one of the partners has died and the other wants to use the embryo post humus of the other partner. In the majority of divorce cases, it has been ruled that the right not to procreate is deemed more important than the right to procreate. Having said that, as you know with the law, for every rule, there is an exception. The very first thing in each of these cases is that the court of law agrees that the embryo will be treated as property and not a person. If it is deemed a person then that comes under family law and involves a custody argument. Usually, in the case of one of the partners being deceased, the remaining spouse typically gets approval to use the embryo. Your niece's case is different to any of these scenarios. The main thing to focus on is if the clinic agrees she is the legal owner of the embryo. If they agree to that then I can't see why she can't use it.'

'She doesn't have any documentation to support

her parents' approval to use their embryo. Do you foresee this would be an issue?'

'With property, once you give it to someone, you lose the right to choose what that person will do with it. Think of it in terms of a family heirloom. Say your dad gave you his grandfather's watch and you chose to sell it, then he would have no say in whether those were his wishes. He no longer has a claim over that property as it would now belong to you. If her parents did not give express instructions in the will as to what was to be done with the frozen embryo and it was not excluded as part of their estate, then it is your niece's decision as to what she wants to do with it.'

'One last question. If she proceeds with having this baby, will there be any legal issues with her relationship to the child? Obviously, they were conceived at the same time which would normally make them twins, but if she gives birth, would she legally be viewed as a sibling or its mother?'

'Genetically, they would be siblings, but legally, if she gives birth to the child then she would be the mother. The same as if she donated the egg to another woman and that woman gave birth, she would legally be the child's mother, even though there is no shared DNA. You know it just occurred to me that if she gives birth to her biological sibling, there might be grounds that half her inheritance could legally belong to the baby. There was a case recently in the USA where the father of frozen embryos sued against an estate, claiming these embryos should have the right to property of his late mother who had a clause in her will that 'surviving' grandchildren would share in $1 million dollars when they turned 25. The father wanted to ensure there was a scope that any unborn children could make a claim against this will. I will email you links to that case and any other cases that I think will be relevant.'

'Thanks for your time, Phil,' Alex said, rising to leave.

'Mate, although legally my opinion is that she has the right to have that child, don't you feel a bit awkward that science has led to such dysfunctional families?'

'I feel really weird about my niece giving birth to her sibling and I'm sure Jody is going to have a fit when she hears about it, but it's not my decision, so I'm going to try to stay out of it,' Alex said, shrugging his shoulders.

'Keep me posted. It is an interesting scenario. Maybe we might have to sue the clinic and create legal history,' Phil said, shaking hands with Alex.

CHAPTER 22

Tiffany nervously paced the hallway outside the clinic doors. She had been invited to make a submission to the ethics committee regarding the possible implantation of the frozen embryo. She quietly mumbled her prepared speech, reciting it over and over. She always got anxious before giving a speech, but this wasn't a university assignment, this was going to affect her whole life.

Looking at her watch once more, Tiffany decided to enter the reception area of Gibson's Clinic. It was after trading hours and the waiting room was unnervingly quiet. The receptionist glanced up at her, registering her arrival with a curt nod. Tiffany sat down, jamming her hands under her thighs to keep them from shaking.

The intercom buzzed and after a moment, the receptionist ushered Tiffany into the boardroom. Tiffany walked to the vacant seat at the top of the table. She looked at the committee of eight men and one woman, who wore expressions ranging from boredom to outright annoyance.

Dr Gibson rose with a file in hand. 'This is Ms Tiffany Parker,' he said in a monotone voice whilst peering over the bi-focal glasses on the end of his nose. 'Her parents, Sandra and David Parker, did IVF through our clinic in 1996. Ms Parker was the only live birth from this treatment. There is one remaining frozen embryo. Ms Parker's parents both died in 2016 and left no instruction as to the action they wanted in regards to this embryo. Ms Parker visited me four weeks ago enquiring about having this embryo, her biological twin, implanted in her.' The committee took notes as Dr Gibson droned on.

'I strongly disagree that it would be considered ethical for a woman to give birth to her genetic twin. I remind you all that incest is illegal. If a woman may not marry a genetically linked sibling, then I am comfortable in us agreeing that she should not be able to give birth to it. I think the only reasonable options for Ms Parker are to donate the embryo to another infertile couple, donate it for scientific research, or dispose of it. Ms Parker is 19 years old and will have many opportunities to have a child that is biologically hers in the years ahead. There is no medical reason why she needs to have this embryo implanted in her and I personally have a conscientious objection to proceeding with this request.' A few of Dr Gibson's colleagues nodded their heads in agreement.

Dr Gibson sat heavily. 'You may speak now, if

you wish, Ms Parker.'

'Thank you all for your time tonight. As Dr Gibson said, I'm Tiffany Parker. I'm nineteen and I'm an orphan. I know my parents may just be a number in your system, but to me, they were my whole world. I hope that none of you ever have to experience the magnitude of grief that I have endured for the last year. It took me a long time to come to terms with my parents' deaths and, to be honest, I don't think it is something that will ever stop haunting me. My parents never made the decision to donate or destroy this remaining embryo and so I know their wishes were not to do either of those things. Family means the world to me, so if I could give birth to the child that my parents struggled to conceive, then I want to do that. I won't agree to kill my sibling, nor use it for a science experiment or be raised in a stranger's family. I want to have the right to give my sibling a life with me where it will be loved and cherished.' She hoped her heartfelt speech would break through the committee members' emotions and they could be swayed from their boss' opinion.

'Everyday, you deal with people using donated eggs that aren't theirs biologically. I don't think my request is any different to that. I have been given legal advice that the embryo is my property. You certainly accept payment from me to keep it frozen every year. It is my right to choose what to do with this embryo and if I choose to have it implanted in me, then I implore you to carry out my wishes.'

A gentleman in a grey suit interrupted, 'Can I just clarify something? Did you and your parents ever discuss the existence of the frozen embryo and why they had continued to freeze it?'

'No. I only learned of the embryo's existence a few months ago,' Tiffany replied.

'Why don't you want to just have your own baby? There are plenty of sperm donors if you don't have a partner,' the only lady panel member contributed.

'This is not about wanting *a* baby, it is about wanting *this* baby. I know the odds are stacked against me in it being viable but I don't think I could live with myself if I didn't at least try to give life to this child.'

'My greatest concern is the emotional wellbeing of the child. It will grow up in a very confusing environment if its sister is its mother and it has no father,' another doctor chimed in.

An older member interjected, 'I am more concerned about your mental health. It seems to me that your grief is the overriding factor in your choice to progress with this procedure. I believe that you may live to regret this decision in the future.'

The lady doctor joined the conversation once more. 'Do you financially have the means to have this procedure and then raise this child?'

Tiffany felt relieved that at last she had been asked a question about logistics, rather than based upon biased opinion. 'Yes. I inherited a sizeable estate from my parents. I'm confident that I have sufficient funds to not only pay for treatment to give birth to this child, but that we will both have a comfortable lifestyle in the future.'

'That may be the case, Ms Parker,' Dr Gibson interrupted, 'however, most single parents have the support network of their parents and siblings and you have made it abundantly clear that you lack that infrastructure. I'm not convinced it would be in either yours or the baby's best interests to proceed. Are there any more queries from the committee members for Ms Parker before we vote?' All the participants sat quietly. 'Ms Parker, the outcome will be based upon a majority vote, not a unanimous vote. Can you please wait in the reception area whilst we take that poll?'

Tiffany stood at her full height, head up, shoulders back and walked purposefully to the waiting room. It was not that she felt in the slightest bit confident; it was just that she endeavoured to portray that she was through her body language. Once she was summoned to join the meeting once more, she entered the room for the verdict. She noted that none of the doctors attempted to make eye contact with her, so without being told the outcome, she knew the result in her gut.

'I'm sorry, Ms Parker,' Dr Gibson said in his patronizing voice, 'the ethics committee have made a determination that the implantation of your parents' frozen embryo in you, its biological sibling, is considered unethical and we will not proceed with this process. You will need to make a decision as to whether you plan to destroy the embryo or donate it to science or another family. Thank you for your time.'

Tiffany's lip trembled and her eyes pooled with tears. There was no point left in trying to appear to be in control. She nodded her understanding, not trusting herself to speak and quickly left the room. She rushed into the ladies toilets and began sobbing for the sibling she would never know and the end to the possibility of any immediate family. The lady doctor from the committee entered the bathroom and Tiffany turned on the tap to splash water on her face. She didn't need further humiliation.

Rubbing her back lightly, the doctor spoke gently, 'I'm sorry you didn't get the result you were after. If it is any consolation, I voted to let you go ahead with the procedure. I think you handled yourself very well in what I know would have been a very intimidating situation for you.' She turned on the tap and rinsed her hands. As she dried them on a paper towel, she whispered to Tiffany, 'Not that I said this to you, but there have been cases where people have sued the practice and a court of law has over-ruled the ethics committee in favour of them.' Returning to her normal voice as she opened the door, she spoke over her shoulder. 'Anyway, Tiffany, don't be too disheartened. You are still young and have the whole world at your feet. Good luck in your future.'

As the door slammed behind the doctor, Tiffany looked at her own reflection in the mirror. Behind the red-rimmed eyes and smudged mascara, she could see a strong, determined person. She knew she was a fighter and a person capable of handling the stress of suing the clinic. Her motto after living the past year in hell was "what doesn't kill you makes you stronger." Without any hesitation, she knew what her next step must be and she knew the first thing she needed to do was contact her uncle's colleague, Phil.

CHAPTER 23

Sitting on the steps of Manly Beach, Tiffany impatiently waited to see Gabby. They say absence makes the heart grow fonder and Tiffany was excited to see her best friend. So much had happened in the past few weeks. She couldn't wait to give Gabby a hug; craving the closeness of the friendship they had shared in school. Two hands covered her eyes from behind. Peeling her friend's hands from her eyes, Tiffany stood up to embrace Gabby.

'How are you?' Gabby asked, squeezing Tiffany hard.

'I'm good. How are you? How was your holiday?'

'It was amazing. Tiff, you've definitely got to come back with me next year. I'm planning a trip through Europe next July. It was incredible in winter, but they say it is even better in summer. Will you come with me?'

Tiffany looked at Gabby with her head cocked, 'I don't think I'll be able to.'

'Come on, Tiff, it will be great! We can cruise around the Mediterranean, trek through the Alps, drink champagne in France and eat pizza in Italy. It will be a trip of a lifetime.'

'It does sound incredible, but I'm planning on having a baby next year.'

'Are you still thinking about doing that? I thought you might have changed your mind. Why don't you postpone that and come live your life a bit before you settle down with a child?'

'Gabby, each year I postpone it, the older the embryo becomes and the less viable it will be. The oldest implanted embryo was 24 years old and mine is already over 20 years old. I need to focus my energy on suing the clinic and getting this baby implanted.'

'Tiff, you know you're my best friend and I'm not saying this to hurt you, but I think it would be a mistake. I think you should wait and have a baby that is naturally conceived; one that is biologically your child, not your sibling.'

All the excitement of seeing Gabby drained away instantly. Tiffany felt betrayed by Gabby's declaration. 'Gab, this is really important to me. I've already set the ball in motion. I want to give this child life.'

'Babe, it's all just a bit weird. I don't think your parents would want this for you. They would want you out living life to the fullest, travelling the world and falling in love, not home changing nappies of a baby that they gave up on years ago.'

Tiffany became defensive, 'Just because my Mum didn't think she would be able to carry the baby, doesn't mean they gave up on it. They preserved it for a reason. I'm going to make sure that it wasn't kept in vain. Look, you might not like my choices but don't ask me to change my mind.'

Gabby shrugged her shoulders, 'It's your life. I just wish you'd start living it a bit.'

'Gabby, I hope you are just jet-lagged because, honestly, you are being really offensive. I'm going to go. I'll catch up with you another time.'

Gabby reached out, 'Tiff, I'm sorry. I don't want you to hate me, but I'd hate myself if I wasn't truthful with you. That's what friends are for.'

'No, Gabby, friends are there to support one another, not tear them down.' Feeling tears pricking her eyes, Tiffany turned before her friend could see her despair. She knew most people would think she was making a stupid mistake, but she didn't think her parents would disapprove. Tiffany decided she should visit her parents' graves. She may not find answers but she would feel a sense of peace being near them.

Tiffany lay in the sun with her eyes closed, strategically placed between the plots of her mum and dad's graves.

'I wish I could speak to you. I'd love to know

what you think of me fighting to give life to my sibling that has been frozen in time. Am I crazy? Would you support me or would you tell me to move on? I miss you both so much and I just want a family again. If I proceed with suing the clinic, then I'm sure that the tabloids will have a field day with me, but at the same time, you both raised me to fight for what I believe in.'

A dark shadow fell over Tiffany. She opened her eyes to find Harley Jefferson standing over her with a sheepish look on his face.

Tiffany gave a little shriek, startled by his presence. She sat bolt upright. 'Oh my God, you nearly gave me a heart attack. You shouldn't sneak up on people.'

'Sorry,' Harley said sincerely. 'I did try to make noise as I approached, but you were busy talking away.'

'Were you eavesdropping on my personal conversation with my parents?'

'Not purposely, but I did hear you say something about suing someone. Is everything okay with you?'

'Are you serious? You are the last person in the world I would share my problems with. You're the one that created all my problems in the first place.'

Harley cast his eyes downward. 'You know that I'm sorry about the accident. If there was any way I could change the events, I would. I would even happily swap places with your parents. You know I don't have to visit your parents' graves, it's not like it is part of my good behaviour bond. I hope you realise I come here because I am truly remorseful.'

Harley removed a withered bunch of flowers from Tiffany's mother's grave and replaced it with a fresh bunch.

'That's another thing. Can you stop bringing flowers to the grave? It makes me feel like a crap daughter when I get here and see fresh flowers. It makes me think that you are more attentive to my parents than I am. I have so much shit to deal with at the moment that I don't have lots of spare time to come and tend to my parents' graves.'

'I'm sorry, Tiffany. I didn't realise it bothered you. I am only trying to show respect to them. You know, I also sit and talk with your parents sometimes too. I ask for their forgiveness and I promise them I will try to be a better person.'

Tiffany stared up into Harley's face. She couldn't decide whether he was just a smooth talker or truthful in his declaration. She knew she would never forgive him. Hating him was far easier than feeling sorry for him, but her multiple spontaneous interactions with him at the cemetery had left her feeling an unexpected pity for his situation. She knew he didn't have to come to her parents' graves and, in fact, she would prefer he didn't, but he chose to visit of his own accord and she could see the importance of this action to him as part of paying his penance.

'Do you have any siblings?' Tiffany asked Harley.

Harley sat down on the grass. 'I have a younger sister, Kayla. She is about a year younger than you.'

'Are you close?'

'We used to really get on each other's nerves when we were kids, but since the accident, our whole family is a lot closer. My family has been so supportive of me. They never yelled at me for being an idiot – which I was. That night, I didn't feel drunk. I honestly thought I would be under the limit, but obviously, I wasn't. As my Mum says, 'Teenage boys always feel invincible.' My parents are now really protective of both my sister and me. I hate that Kayla has had to live with the shame of having a brother that killed three people. I know secretly she must hate the fact that my parents won't let her be a passenger in a car driven by someone who has had a single drink, but she never whines about it. We all know too well that teenage drivers are inexperienced and that tragic accidents can happen.'

'How did Kayla react when she heard about the accident?'

'I will never forget the expression on her face when I told her what had happened, after I came home from the police station with Mum and Dad. She went white and crumpled into a ball, crying harder than anyone I've ever seen in my life. She used to idolize Tia and she couldn't believe that she had also been killed in the accident along with your innocent parents. She kept asking over and over whether I would be going to jail.' Harley's lip trembled and he turned his face away from Tiffany.

Tiffany's memory jumped back to the morning she was told of the accident and she knew the description that Harley had given of his sister's reaction was only slightly less than her own reaction to finding out both her parents were dead.

'So, I guess she was pretty relieved that you got off so lightly.' Tiffany said to the back of Harley's head.

'Yes, my family were relieved I didn't go to jail. You know, you take your family for granted until there is a chance that you won't be around them anymore. I guess I don't need to tell you that, you know it better than anyone else. My sister always has my back and I honestly would be lost without her support. I realise you believe I got off lightly, but I don't think you understand that any sentence I might have been given from the court pales into insignificance in comparison to the fact that I have a life sentence of hating myself.'

Tiffany stared at the ground looking contrite. Under normal circumstances, Tiffany would have comforted a person who was suffering such inner turmoil, but she couldn't bring herself to console the guy who had killed her parents. If anything, he should be consoling her!

'I'm not sure if you are interested to know, but I am involved in a drink-driving education course and have started visiting high-schools to educate kids on the effects of alcohol and speeding when driving.' Tiffany reflected back on seeing Harley at the high school she had visited. At least the mystery of what he was doing there was now solved.

'I figure if my story can stop another kid making a stupid choice of getting behind the wheel after a drink, then there has been a small amount of good that has come from the situation. I'm training to be a teacher and I just want to help protect kids from themselves.'

Tiffany nodded as she took in Harley's earnestness. She found her emotions confusing. She wanted to hate him with all her heart but having him confide his torment to her meant her hate was beginning to thaw.

'Anyway, I've got to go. My mum is waiting in the car. I'm sorry I intruded on your time here. Would you like me to take my bunch of flowers away?' Harley asked as he rose to leave.

'No, you might as well leave them since you already bought them. Just don't buy flowers anymore, okay?' Tiffany said in a sulky voice.

'Okay. Well, take care. I'll see you around.'

'Bye,' Tiffany said quietly.

After watching Harley's retreating figure walk slowly back to the car park, Tiffany's thoughts returned to the conversation she'd been having with her parents before he arrived. Should she fight to have her sibling? Her short discussion with Harley had clarified her thoughts that siblings should look out for each other. They have an innate responsibility to protect and care for one another. Although her discussion with Harley was not about her dilemma, it had shed light on her decision in an unexpected way.

CHAPTER 24

Sitting across the desk from Phil Saunders, Tiffany was advised that the letter of demand sent to Gibson's Clinic had been formally rejected and that a statement of claim had now been filed with the court. Tiffany was overwhelmed with the amount of information Phil was trying to gather for her case. He had warned her before they started that he would be delving into a lot of personal information, as he had to know anything that may come to light under cross-examination. His questions came in rapid fire:

Did she have a copy of her birth certificate, her parents' will and paperwork to prove her ownership of the trust fund?

Had her parents ever discussed wanting a sibling for her?

Had she ever told her parents she wanted a sibling?

Had her parents ever suggested they did not want to donate the embryo to science?

Had her parents ever suggested they did not want to donate the embryo to another family?

Had her parents ever suggested they did not want to destroy the embryo?

Had her parents ever talked about their will with her?

Why did it take over a year from inheriting the embryo to meet with the clinic?

What was her mental health like?

Had she ever suffered a mental health problem?

Did she drink and do drugs?

Did she have a criminal record?

Did she know if she was fertile?

Had she ever been pregnant?

Had she ever had a sexually transmitted disease?

Had she ever expressed a desire to have a child at such a young age?

Had she ever been responsible for caring for a child?

How did she cope with needles?

How much money did she have?

How was that money invested?

Had she obtained a professional opinion that her inheritance would provide sufficient funds to raise a child?

What interests and hobbies did she have?

How intensive was her university course?

What were her plans for completing her university course if she had a child?

What were her plans after graduating university?

Did she have a partner?

Was she promiscuous?

What people would be in her life to support her?

Were there people in her social set with a criminal record?

Did she drive?

What was her driving record like?

What was her diet like?

Did she exercise?

Where would she live if she had a baby?

What plans had she considered for educating a child?

Tiffany massaged her temples in a futile effort to relieve the tension headache that felt like a clamp on her skull. Eventually, after three hours of quizzing Tiffany, Phil finally started discussing his plans for the case.

'Tiffany, I believe we have good cause to believe that you should win this case. There is precedence in cases heard in America where frozen embryos have been deemed property and not a person. With this being the case, it should be up to you what you choose to do with your property. I will subpoena a copy of the original contract your parents signed with the Gibson's Clinic, your mother's medical records, your patient records from your GP and psychiatrist. Once I have all those, I will be able to see if there are any clauses or loopholes the defence will try to use in the case.'

'I have a question. Is it illegal for a doctor to choose not to treat a patient?'

'A doctor takes an oath to do no harm, so if there was a medical emergency then they cannot refuse to help. They also can't refuse to treat someone based on religious, political or racial reasons. However, they can make a conscientious objection and refuse to treat a person if there is someone else available that is willing to treat that patient. Tiffany, your case is a bit different to most medical cases as you don't technically have a health issue requiring treatment.'

'There is a woman doctor at the clinic who told me she voted for me to be allowed to use the embryo. Couldn't they just let her do the procedure?'

'Their board of ethics does not want anyone in the practice doing the procedure. You have to understand this is very controversial. You have to be prepared for your name to be dragged through the mud. They will try to say not only is it unethical as you are biological twins, but I believe they will also try to suggest you are incapable of being a good mother. The press will probably have a field day. This case is unique as there aren't that many frozen embryos that have been kept long enough to be implanted in an adult sibling. Whatever the result, it will be ground-breaking. The law in regards to the entities that are frozen embryos is vague. It is only in recent years, clinics have started suggesting to patients that they should make provisions for what should happen with their frozen eggs, sperm and embryos in the case of divorce or death. Your parents were way before that time, which is why this oversight occurred. You need to be prepared to be ridiculed, judged and harassed when this case goes to court.'

Tiffany's stomach was in knots. She knew that if she weren't fully committed, she would become derailed. 'I don't care what people say about me. I'm doing what feels right in my gut. As you said earlier, it's my property and my decision. People have no right to tell me how to live my life. Unless you have walked in someone else's shoes, you don't know how you would behave in any given situation. I'm committed to this, even if people think I'm crazy.'

'Okay, Tiffany, I think that we have covered all that we needed to today. I will arrange to subpoena those documents. This is going to be a lengthy process, so you need to make sure you look after yourself.'

'Thanks, Phil,' Tiffany said, standing and shaking his hand.

CHAPTER 25

The stress of suing a medical clinic whilst trying to complete her next semester of university took its toll on Tiffany. She found herself struggling to sleep, her thoughts cycling over and over as she lay in the darkness. When her skin broke out in an itchy red rash, she decided to visit her GP. Within a few minutes of discussing her condition, she was given a script for a cortisone cream and advised she should visit a psychiatrist for some counselling.

Sitting on the soft leather couch in Dr Flanders office brought back a myriad of memories of the months just after her parents passed away.

'Hi, Tiffany. It's lovely to see you. I last saw you in July last year. What has been going on in your life since then?'

'I took your advice. I gathered up all the letters I had written to my parents and I took them on a trip to Fiji. One night, I read each letter and then burnt it.'

'How did you feel after that?' Dr Flanders asked.

'I felt better; lighter.'

'That is great to hear. You made such great progress with your grief. So, what is going on in your life now?'

'Well, after my trip, I took over managing the trust fund set up from my parents' estate. Up to that point, I had maintained it just as my uncle had set it up for me. Late last year, I decided to go through my parents' possessions and reduce what was in storage. It was liberating. After that, I looked at all the suppliers as I was paying for services that I didn't even know what they were and I discovered my parents had a frozen embryo from when they did their course of IVF to have me.'

Dr Flanders leaned forward. 'What did you decide to do with that? I can imagine it was difficult for you to destroy it after the deaths of your parents.'

'I have decided to have it implanted and give it life. My parents never destroyed it, so I couldn't do that either with a clear conscience.'

'I assume you've considered donating the embryo?'

'Of course, but if that had been my parents' wishes, they would have done that years ago. You know better than most people that family means the world to me. I want this child to live and be loved. I want my family back and I know I can't bring back my parents, but I can start my sibling's life.' Tiffany reached for a tissue to dab her eyes. Talking to a non-judgmental person made her feel emotional.

'It sounds like you've made up your mind. When are you having the procedure?'

'The clinic has refused my request to implant the embryo and I'm now suing them.'

'I see,' Dr Flanders responded quietly.

'My stress levels are through the roof. I have uni exams coming up, I've had a falling out with my best friend because she thinks I'm crazy and I haven't had a full night's sleep in weeks. I just lie awake thinking of all the things people have said about my choice. I question what my parents would have thought. I wonder whether I will win this case or if I'm just throwing away money. Most of all, I worry that even if I'm successful in winning the case, the embryo might not take and it will all be for nothing.'

'I can tell you're stressed. Just take a few deep breaths to calm down.'

Tiffany took a few deep breaths as per the exercise she had done after her previous visits with Dr Flanders.

'You know the body doesn't function properly without sleep. You become agitated, angry and more stressed. That stress then stops you from sleeping properly and it becomes a vicious cycle. I would like to prescribe you some mild sleeping tablets to take for a few weeks. You can then wean yourself off them. It is important to get you into a normal sleep cycle again. I also think that you are taking on too much. I would suggest you defer at least one course at university for this semester. You won't be able to give all your subjects your best effort under the pressure you are feeling at the moment.'

'What do you think about me giving birth to my sibling? Do you think it makes me crazy?' Tiffany asked curiously.

'Tiffany, I can tell you categorically that you are not crazy. What you want to do is unorthodox but that doesn't mean it is wrong. It is not my place to tell you how to live your life. I'm just here to help you cope with living your life.'

'Thanks, Grace. It is so nice to be able to talk to someone who isn't going to judge me. I truly think I probably would have gone insane last year if it hadn't been for your help.'

'I'm glad I was able to help. How are you coping now with the loss of your parents?'

'I miss them every day. I visit their graves regularly. The weirdest thing is that the guy that was responsible for the accident visits their graves all the time too. I have bumped into him there a few times.'

'How did you handle that?'

'I want to hate him for killing my parents. I did hate him for a long time. I was so angry that he got off so lightly, but when I've spoken to him, he seems really remorseful. It feels disloyal to my parents to not hate him, but I have started to feel sorry for him. I'm sure that he never meant to kill my parents and his girlfriend. He actually seems pretty tormented by the accident.'

'I think it is very mature of you to feel empathy for him. Of course, it is a very normal reaction to feel resentment towards the person who was responsible for the death of your parents, but hating him won't bring them back. I'm sure your parents would prefer you didn't harbour a grudge. It seems that part of his journey to reconciling his actions may be trying to do the virtuous thing by visiting their resting place.'

'I get that, but still, I find it kind of creepy.'

'If he finds peace from visiting the graves of the people he was responsible for killing then I don't think you should find it creepy. You should respect that he is taking accountability for his actions.'

CHAPTER 26

With the help of sleeping tablets and having deferred the subjects she was doing for her law degree for the semester, Tiffany felt as if a small weight had been lifted off her shoulders. She had time to concentrate on her communication assignments, as well as prepare herself for the onslaught of the trial.

Whilst finalising the conclusion for her latest assessment, Tiffany was interrupted by the quiet buzz of her phone vibrating on the hard wood of her compact desk. Any time she saw Phil's phone number appear, her pulse began to race.

'Hi, Tiffany. I just wanted to update you on a few things in regards to your case. The date has been set for three weeks' time. I have reviewed the subpoenaed files and they have highlighted a few areas of concern. Firstly, the original contract your parents' signed with Gibson's Clinic had a clause that in layman's terms states the frozen embryo may only be implanted in their clinic. Your parents agreed to that, so it may inhibit requesting the embryo be used at another facility. Secondly, the records from your psychiatrist note that you were suffering treatment for depression, which the other side may use against you to prove you suffer from a mental illness. It also states you have recently been prescribed sleeping tablets, which they might say proves you have a reliance on drugs. None of these are major issues, but I wanted you to know about them, so they don't come as a surprise in court.'

'I thought my files with Dr Flanders were considered confidential,' Tiffany said, horrified at the way the facts might be twisted.

'They are unless they are subpoenaed for a court of law. Are you still taking the sleeping tablets?'

'I only take half a tablet a night. The stress of everything over the past year has affected my sleep. I only take them so I feel rested and can cope with the pressure I'm under,' Tiffany said, trying to defend herself. 'I can't believe they might say I have a mental illness because I was depressed after both my parents were killed suddenly. Wouldn't you have a mental illness if you weren't depressed under those circumstances?'

'Tiffany, you can calm down. These issues can all be explained away, although I would recommend you stop taking the sleeping tablets if you can. I don't want it to appear that you have a drug dependency.'

'Okay,' Tiffany said, resigned to surrendering to

his request.

'Finally, I want to recommend you hire a barrister to represent you in court. I have a lot of experience in family law courts, but as this case is ground-breaking, I think you would be better served to use a barrister. They are expensive, but it may be the difference between winning and losing the case. I'm pretty certain Gibson will have hired a barrister to represent him.'

'Okay. Who do I hire?' Tiffany asked.

'Mark Reidy is a very good barrister with a great track record. I know he has had previous experience in frozen reproduction cases. I am happy to brief him on this case on your behalf if you like.'

'Thanks, Phil. I just want to do whatever it takes to win this case.'

On the first day of the trial, Tiffany walked into court, looking as confident and mature as possible. She knew first impressions counted and she wanted the judge to not only agree she had the right to implant the embryo but also that she was fit to care for a child.

The courtroom was stuffy and wood panelled; similar to the room in which she had sat for weeks listening to the case regarding her parents' deaths. That trial she had felt hopeless and alone, this trial gave her a glimmer of hope that she needn't stay that way.

After the formalities of the judge entering the court, the judge requested the plaintiff's barrister state his case.

Mark stood to address the judge. 'Your Honour, my client, Ms Tiffany Parker, is the only child of Sandra and David Parker and was conceived by IVF in 1997 through Gibson's Clinic. Ms Parker's parents both died in a tragic car accident in November 2015, leaving Ms Parker an orphan and sole beneficiary to their estate. One item of property she inherited was a frozen embryo that has been stored at Gibson's Clinic since conception. Since inheriting this embryo, Ms Parker has continued to pay an annual fee to keep the embryo frozen. In February 2017, Ms Parker made a request to Gibson's Clinic to have the lone embryo implanted in her. She was denied approval to undertake this procedure by the board of Gibson's Clinic citing ethical reasons. There is no denying the embryo is Ms Parker's property. Dr Arthur Gibson has, on several occasions, told Ms Parker she has to make the decision to either terminate the embryo or donate it to another family or to science. If she has the right to decide what to do with her property, then it is not Dr Gibson's right to make that decision on her behalf. The Gibson Clinic does over 100 implantations of donated embryos into their patients each year. That is where a couple is not biologically linked to the embryo. My client, Ms Parker, wants the right to have her parents' embryo implanted in her, just as these other couples have other people's embryos implanted in them. It is her property and her decision. The fact that she is biologically from the same parents should work in her favour as she should be biologically compatible to carry this baby. This embryo is her blood relative and who better to raise this child than someone related to it.

'Your Honour, Dr Gibson implied to Ms Parker at the meeting of the ethics committee for Gibson's Clinic, that what she wanted to do should be classified as incest. I want to debunk this ridiculous notion before the defence wastes any of your time. Incest is an illegal act of related persons having sexual interaction. My client wants to give birth to a child, not molest it.

'I understand this case is unique, but I hope the theatrics that the defence will bring to the table will not distract you from the core issue of the case. The frozen embryo is Ms Parker's property and what she does with it is her choice.

'Thank you.'

The judge sat with pen in hand scribbling notes on a legal pad. After a few minutes, he motioned for the defendant's barrister to start his opening statement.

'Your Honour, what sort of perverse society are we creating where someone can give birth to their twin? Just because it is scientifically possible, doesn't make it right. Ms Parker may have inherited the frozen embryo, but she has no written consent from her parents that they would agree to her foolishness to give birth to their child. In fact, Ms Parker didn't even know of the embryo's existence until late last year. Don't you think if her parents would have been supportive of her giving birth to her twin that a simple discussion may have been had some time in the eighteen years they lived with her? We have no proof that this procedure is what the biological parents would have wanted. We don't believe Ms Parker is in the right frame of mind to go through with this process, as it is not a decision that should be made on a whim, especially when suffering mental illness. Ms Parker's psychiatrist has documented that Ms Parker has suffered depression since the deaths of her parents. Is it sensible to burden her with the stress of raising a baby as an only parent, when she clearly isn't coping already without that added responsibility? Further, we believe it is definitely not in the baby's best interest to be born into such a dysfunctional family situation. Does Ms Parker want to be this child's mother or sister? We have sourced a professional psychological opinion that believes that if this child were to be born, it would suffer mental anguish being birthed by its twin. Finally, and it is a complex situation to grapple with, if this child is born, it is legally a surviving heir to the estate that Ms Parker inherited. Sandra and David Parker's will reads, and I quote, "all property will be equally divided between any surviving children." Therefore, this future child which would have survived its biological parents, would have the right to half of the estate, meaning that it would also have the right to choose what to have done with the frozen embryo that was part of the estate upon its parents' death. Therefore, hypothetically, this child could sue Ms Parker and Gibson's Clinic for not getting its consent to use the embryo, as it would legally own the embryo as much as Ms Parker does.

'Does this unborn child have rights? Do we need to suspend any action on the embryo to save ourselves from future litigation? These are murky waters in which we wade.

'Your Honour, as this case will set a precedence, I ask you to consider, not only if the frozen embryo is Ms Parker's property, but the implications on the nation if this perverse implantation was allowed to proceed.

'Thank you.'

Tiffany felt her face heat up as a blush flooded her cheeks. She was being portrayed as a mentally ill pervert. She made eye contact with the court illustrator who was staring at her features, sketching a portrait to splash across the media. She averted her eyes and had a sip of water.

The judge adjourned the court until the following day. As Tiffany walked out into the street accompanied by her legal team, she was set upon by a pack of journalists. 'Tiffany,' they yelled at her, firing questions in rapid succession.

'Why do you want to give birth to your twin?'

'Do you think your parents would approve?'

'Do you want to be its mother or sister?'

Tiffany shielded her face whilst Phil guided her towards her car. 'We have no comment at this time,' Phil repeated to several persistent reporters who continued to shove microphones in front of them.

Inside the sanctuary of her car, Tiffany held her hands out in front of her, surprised by how hard they were shaking. She had been warned that the case would create interest, but she had not been prepared to be set upon by a pack of heartless media.

Not bothering to turn her phone on after the day in court, Tiffany drove directly to the cemetery, where she hoped to find peace and quiet. As she walked towards her parents' graves, she could see the silhouette of someone standing by them. As she got closer, she realised that Harley was standing in quiet contemplation. She had assumed that he had stopped visiting their graves as she hadn't seen any flowers near the headstones since she last saw Harley.

Harley turned towards Tiffany as she approached. 'Hey.'

'Hi,' Tiffany said shyly.

'I heard all about you on the news headlines on the radio this afternoon. You're famous!'

'That got out quick,' Tiffany said, shocked that her case was featuring on the news.

'I know how you must be feeling. Do you remember when my court case was on and I had journalists harassing my family and me every day for weeks? I felt like a dirty criminal.'

'Yeah, it's pretty confronting,' Tiffany agreed.

'So, you really want to give birth to your twin?' Harley asked, his eyebrows raised.

'Yes. I miss my family and I want to be able to give life to this child that has been frozen in limbo for too long. Family means the world to me and I want to mean the world to this child.'

'You're brave,' Harley said, looking down at Sandra's grave. 'I certainly wouldn't be ready to take on the responsibility of raising a child.'

'Well, I sort of already have that responsibility of looking after myself since I don't have any family. I don't think it will be that big a leap in responsibility. You know I'm not a real party girl. I just crave the comfort of a home to share with my loved ones.'

'You know that I'm on home detention, but I don't really miss the party scene. I'm super close with my family now and it's a relaxed and caring environment to be in. Don't get me wrong, I can't wait for my home detention to be over to gain my independence again, but I actually like hanging out with my family.'

'Your mum is really protective,' Tiffany said, reflecting back on her interactions with Mrs Jefferson.

'That's what makes her a good mum. I would bet that if you have this baby, you will be super protective of it too.'

'Yeah, I guess you're right.'

'Anyway, talking of Mum, I have to go. She is waiting in the car.'

'I'll walk with you,' Tiffany replied, 'it's getting too cold to stand here. I'll come back another time.'

As they walked in companionable silence towards the car park, suddenly, Harley grabbed Tiffany's arm. 'There's a photographer waiting by your car and what looks like a news van parked a bit further up. How about I get Mum to drive around to the side street to get you out of here? You can come back to our house and Mum can drop you back later when they have left.'

Tiffany felt awkward accepting Harley's offer, but it was the lesser of two evils. She couldn't stand the thought of being pestered by journalists; giving them more fodder for the evening news.

'Okay, if that is alright with your Mum,' Tiffany responded sheepishly.

Harley phoned his mum to make arrangements. He lightly put his hand on the small of Tiffany's back and directed her towards the meeting point.

As they neared Harley's Mum's car, Tiffany felt anxious. The only verbal interaction she had ever had with Mrs Jefferson was an outburst in the foyer of the court.

Harley opened the car door and ushered Tiffany into the back seat of the car.

'Hello, Tiffany,' Mrs Jefferson said, smiling in Tiffany's direction.

'Thank you for helping me, Mrs Jefferson. I can't believe the media have the hide to stalk me at the cemetery.'

'Please call me Cathy. The media is unscrupulous; they will do anything to get a story. When Harley was first on home detention, I would be hanging out the washing in the back yard and find a photographer peering over the fence waiting to get a photo of him. It is such an invasion of privacy.'

Tiffany had been so caught up in the emotion of the trial from her perspective, she had never considered what Harley and his family had gone through.

'You are welcome to stay for dinner tonight and then I can drop you back to your car,' Cathy said, catching Tiffany off guard.

'Thank you, but I don't want to impose,' Tiffany

said politely.

'Do you have other plans?' Harley asked gently.

'No. I just have to get mentally prepared to be made the laughing stock of Sydney again tomorrow,' Tiffany said sarcastically.

'You should stay for dinner. I've eaten at Dunkirk before and the food is very average. Mum is a good cook,' Harley said.

Tiffany was taken aback. She didn't realise Harley knew where she lived. Laughing, Tiffany replied, 'Well, you do have a point. Last night we had some stew type of thing. One of the guys was telling everyone it was made from the rats they found in the kitchen. It put me off eating it.'

Cathy laughed. 'If I promise not to serve you rat stew, would you like to stay for dinner?'

'Okay. If it is not too much trouble that would be nice,' Tiffany said. She shook her head slightly, trying to reconcile being invited to eat dinner with her sworn enemies.

As they drove up a non-descript suburban street in Roseville, Tiffany was surprised by the normalcy of where Harley lived. In her mind, she had pictured him as a spoilt brat from a rich family, living in a mansion by the sea. Cathy pulled into the driveway of a small single storey house. The dwelling was a tidy brick home and the gardens were immaculate.

'Your gardens look beautiful,' Tiffany

complimented Cathy.

'That's all Harley's work. He has to do something to pass the time he is cooped up at home. He has a natural green thumb,' she replied.

The more Tiffany learnt about Harley, the more he seemed to be nothing like the guy she had presumed him to be. She would have assumed he would have spent his time indoors playing PlayStation, not outside gardening for his parents.

'I wouldn't have picked you as a gardener,' Tiffany said to Harley as they got out of the car.

'It's only a small token to thank my parents for their support. My court case cost them all their savings, plus they had to take a mortgage out on their home. I will never be able to repay them.'

Tiffany nodded. She knew all too well the huge expense of legal cases.

As Cathy opened the front door, a small fluffy brown dog jumped up and down excitedly at their feet. With its tail wagging at a rapid pace, it was clear that it adored its owners.

Harley scooped up the little dog and held it close to his chest, while it wriggled madly, trying to lick his face. 'This is Ruby,' he said, patting the dog's head tenderly.

Tiffany tickled the dog under the chin, 'Hello, Ruby, aren't you a cutie!'

'Why don't you guys watch some television

while I make dinner,' Cathy said, walking towards the kitchen.

'Can I help you, Cathy?' Tiffany asked to her retreating back.

'No, just entertain Ruby. She's been home by herself for a few hours and she could do with the company.'

Tiffany followed Harley into the lounge room. 'I feel kind of weird being here,' Tiffany said as she sat on a single lounge chair.

'Good, because I feel kind of weird you being here,' Harley joked. He turned on the television quietly in the background to offer a welcome distraction. 'What do you want to watch?'

'Anything but the news,' Tiffany said, leaning down to pat Ruby's back.

Harley surfed the channels, finally deciding upon an old episode of Family Feud. Tiffany would never have chosen to watch this television show, but its light-hearted banter was just what she needed after the stressful day she'd had.

The front door slammed and a loud voice boomed through the house, 'You guys won't believe what I just heard on the radio! You know Tiffany Parker, apparently she ...' Kayla, Harley's sister, bound into the lounge room, dumping her bag in the corner of the room. She stopped suddenly when she saw Tiffany sitting in the chair, with Ruby lying on her back on Tiffany's lap getting tummy rubs.

'Kayla, this is Tiffany,' Harley said, breaking the awkward silence.

'Hi,' Tiffany said, smiling shyly. Kayla looked towards Harley and back to Tiffany again.

'Um, hi,' Kayla said, confusion written on her face.

'Tiffany is staying for dinner,' Harley said to Kayla.

'Right,' Kayla nodded, 'this isn't awkward at all, is it?'

'Only if you make it awkward, Kayla,' Harley said sternly. 'We know about Tiffany's court case. She is here so she could avoid photographers.'

'Cool,' Kayla said, sitting down next to Harley. 'So, is it true you want to give birth to your twin?'

'Kayla, can you give the girl a break? She is here for us to protect her from getting harassed, not to be harassed by you,' Harley said, shaking his head.

'It's okay, Harley. Yes, Kayla, I do want to try to give birth to the frozen embryo that is in storage,' Tiffany said diplomatically. She didn't like to call the embryo her twin as it sensationalized the situation.

'I couldn't think of anything worse than having a baby. I need my beauty sleep too much,' Kayla joked.

'Yeah, we are waiting for it to start working,' Harley joked. Laughing, he ruffled the smooth dark hair on the top of Kayla's head. She rolled her eyes and playfully punched her brother in the arm before she got up to walk to the kitchen.

Harley's dad, Martin, arrived home from work and the look of confusion on his face made Tiffany feel awkward. She smiled sweetly as she was introduced to him. He gave a polite nod of his head before asking Cathy to join him in his study for a moment.

Although the television was on, Tiffany tried to eavesdrop on the conversation that Martin and Cathy were having in the adjacent room.

'What is she doing here? Don't you remember her abusing you in court?' Martin asked, his voice filled with emotion.

'Martin, she is just a young girl that had lost her parents. Don't you think our kids might react the same way if the shoe was on the other foot?'

'Maybe, but that doesn't explain why she is here,' he replied surly.

'Poor Tiffany has been stalked by reporters all day as she is involved in a court case. Do you remember how horrible it was for Harley? How the media were so persistent and had no qualms about getting in his personal space? Harley bumped into Tiffany at the cemetery today and there were reporters waiting at her car to get the scoop of her visiting her dead parents. I picked them up in a side-street so she could avoid being harassed by them. I will drop her back to her car later.' There was a small lull in the conversation and then Cathy spoke again, her voice softer this time so that Tiffany had to strain to hear her comments. 'Martin, she has no-one. She can't rely on her parents to support her through this trying time and the reason she is orphaned is our son's fault. We can't bring her parents back, but we can try to be helpful and supportive. It is the least we can do.'

Cathy was obviously very persuasive because when Tiffany sat with the family at the dinner table, Martin acted as if it was the most natural thing in the world for Tiffany to be sharing a meal with them in their house.

'So, Tiffany, what are you studying at university?' Martin asked as everyone sat quietly at the dining table.

'I'm doing a double degree of law and communications,' Tiffany replied.

'Looks like you are getting good work experience for your law degree with all the time you've spent in the courts over the last few years,' Kayla said cheekily.

'I guess so,' Tiffany said smiling. She found it hard to decipher if Kayla was trying to be funny or whether she harboured a grudge against her.

Tiffany worried that discussing court would open

old wounds and remind them all of the pain and suffering they had all endured throughout Harley's case. 'Actually, I've deferred my law subjects for this semester as I was just too stressed. It will add another semester to the length of my degree, but it seemed like the best thing to do given how I was feeling.' An awkward lull in conversation ensued. The only sounds were cutlery moving on plates.

'So, Tiffany, it looks like you've won a life-long friend in Ruby,' Cathy said.

Tiffany looked at the little fluffy dog sitting by her side. 'Look at those puppy dog eyes. She is so cute.'

'Don't be fooled by her, Tiffany. She's only sitting next to you because she knows she won't get any food from us,' Harley said, laughing.

Having broken the tension, the conversation around the table flowed freely and Tiffany was shocked to find she was feeling at ease in this family situation. She missed having an evening meal with her family and this carefree banter was what she hoped she might achieve if and when she finally had a child.

After the meal, Tiffany helped clear the plates from the table. Standing in the kitchen, Cathy took the plates and stacked them in the dishwasher. 'Would you like me to take you back to your car now? I'm sure the coast is clear. I wonder how long they waited to ambush you?'

'The joke was on them, wasn't it?' Tiffany said, smiling at the thought of them conspiring to outwit the media. 'It would be great if you could drop me back to my car when you're ready.'

'I'll go get my keys,' Cathy said.

Tiffany walked into the living room. 'I'm going to go now. Thank you for having me,' Tiffany said to Martin.

'You're welcome here anytime, Tiffany,' Martin replied.

Harley came and stood beside her. 'Bye, Tiffany. Good luck tomorrow.' He gave her arm a small squeeze.

'Thanks for coming to my rescue today,' Tiffany said solemnly.

'Anytime,' he replied.

Tiffany hurried towards her dorm room, not wanting to be stopped by people giving her their opinions about her court case.

Once within the safety of her room, she flopped down on her bed and turned on her phone. The number of missed phone calls and text messages astonished her. The messages, on the whole, were supportive of her and wished her good luck. She noticed there was a missed call from Gabby but she hadn't left a message. The two of them hadn't spoken since the day they had met at Manly. Gabby had tried calling but Tiffany had been so hurt that she refused to speak to her. Tiffany wished now that she hadn't been so stubborn because, on a day like today, she could have used a friend to confide in.

Out of habit, Tiffany clicked on her Facebook app. She was shocked to see how quickly the world had latched onto her court case. There were online news and magazine articles that discussed the pros and cons of her choice. There were even multiple memes already in circulation. One was showing her birthing a clone of herself; another one was of her grabbing an egg from the freezer. She clicked on a news article and was stunned by the vitriol in the comments. Trolls could be so harsh. Some called her selfish, others referred to her as a freak, while one woman said she deserved to burn in hell. Tiffany switched off her phone once more. It would be hard enough to sleep tonight without these vicious comments looping around in her brain.

CHAPTER 27

Day two of the court case, Tiffany anxiously walked up to the witness box. She sat in the chair with her hands gripping the railing in front of her – white knuckles the only sign of the tension she felt.

A few weeks prior, she had met with Mark to discuss potential questions that may be asked in the witness box. They agreed she should establish the fact that she was an upstanding student and that it was important for the judge to develop empathy for her loss. Most of all, she needed to appear mature and responsible so there was no doubt that she had the ability to raise a child.

Mark read the affidavit aloud to the court. It highlighted how important family was to her, how she had coped with losing both her parents and the excessive stress caused as a result of the court case surrounding their death. The affidavit then reflected upon her university life and how she was coping with her courses. As her evidence was relayed to the court, Tiffany became calmer and more confident that the judge would have to award the case to her.

After four hours of testimony, Mark rested his case.

The assault of questions from the defence was relentless. Tiffany found herself agreeing that she had been depressed after the death of her parents, but she argued that grieving was a normal reaction. She then acknowledged that she had been using sleeping tablets but clarified that it was only for a short period of time to help her cope with stress. The defence barrister then used the words against her to state to the judge that if she can't cope with stress and lack of sleep now, then she surely shouldn't contemplate having a baby. With each response she gave, the barrister managed to twist her words, leaving her feeling humiliated and angry.

By the time the questioning turned to her finances, Tiffany's head ached and she felt emotionally drained. The barrister asked her credentials for managing money, knowing she was only just nineteen without any formal training in investing money. He then badgered her to ask whether, in her opinion, she had enough money to live on and support a child. She agreed that with her inheritance she believed she did. He then queried whether she could make ends meet with only half that money. Unsure where this questioning was going, she replied that she wasn't sure whether only half the money would be enough to make ends meet. The barrister sneered at her then turned to address the judge, stating that upon the birth of the child, it would legally become a second beneficiary to their parents' estate, therefore, half of the money from the estate should go into a trust fund for the child to access upon turning eighteen, as per the terms of Sandra and David Parker's wills.

Tiffany took a deep breath and dug her fingernails into the palms of her hands, leaving small crescent-shaped indents, as she tried to distract herself from her urge to cry. She couldn't look at the stressed face of her barrister or the smug look on the defence barrister's face. Instead, she turned her face to look up at the ceiling. As she lowered her head, she observed the facial expressions of the journalists sitting in the public gallery. She recognised those gleeful looks. She'd seen them before on her schoolmates back in high school, just before they were about to divulge some juicy gossip. Tiffany bet the journalists were eager for today's proceedings to end so they could jostle their way out of the courthouse, all hoping to be the first to file their reports in time for the 6 o'clock news. Just as she went to look away, she caught eye-contact with Cathy Jefferson. She sat in the back corner of the gallery with a look of pity on her face. Tiffany was familiar with that expression too; it was the one Cathy had worn every time she looked at her son throughout his court case the year before.

The judge announced a recess in proceedings and

stated that the case would resume the following morning at 9am. As Tiffany stood for the judge, she watched the pack of media eagerly scamper from the room and she knew that they would be waiting to attack her with microphones and cameras as soon as she left the courthouse.

After empty reassurances from Alex and Phil that today's evidence hadn't been too damning for her case, Tiffany walked the gauntlet through the throng of journalists all calling her name and yelling questions at her. She held her hand in front of her face, trying not to walk into a cameraman walking backwards in front of her or hit her head on a fuzzy grey microphone boom positioned just above her bowed head. She couldn't imagine what it would be like to be famous with paparazzi stalking your every movement. She knew in a few weeks she would be yesterday's news and she hoped that her sanity lasted long enough to deal with this extra pressure at the end of every day at court.

Tiffany was feeling claustrophobic with the crowd all pressing in on her. As she stepped towards the pedestrian crossing, Cathy's white Toyota Corolla pulled up in front of her. With her window down, Cathy called out to Tiffany, 'Do you want a lift?' Without hesitation, Tiffany opened the door of the car and hopped in. It was such a welcome relief when the door closed and Cathy drove away from the chaos of the media.

'That's two days in a row you've saved me from those menaces,' Tiffany said with gratitude.

'I'm glad I could be of assistance,' Cathy said, smiling back at Tiffany.

'Why were you in court today?' Tiffany queried.

'I just wanted to see how you coped. It must be so hard for you to be under such pressure. I know you don't have your parents to rely on and my son is the reason for that, so I've taken it upon myself to look out for you on their behalf.'

Tiffany was touched by Cathy's maternal instinct. 'You know, I'm not your responsibility and I don't hold you accountable for what happened to my parents.'

'I know that, but I can't help but feel that you need someone to lean on and if I can help, then I'm here for you.'

Tiffany turned her face to look out the side window of the car and surreptitiously brushed the back of her hand against her cheek to wipe away a tear that cascaded from her eye.

Over the last few months, Tiffany had felt abandoned. After her falling out with Gabby, Tiffany knew her stubbornness was responsible for the fact that she had lost her best friend, yet she couldn't bring herself to make amends. Her Aunty Jody had even been rather absent over the previous months once it became clear that Tiffany was serious about having the embryo implanted. Without having told her to her face, Tiffany knew her aunty had serious reservations about her niece proceeding with giving birth to her dead sister's child. The only person Tiffany felt she could confide in was Dr Flanders, but it was now clear that even those conversations weren't confidential, as Dr Flanders had been called as a witness in the case. The fact that Cathy was offering Tiffany a non-judgmental olive branch was surprising and comforting at once.

'Do you want to come back to our place for a bit or would you prefer I drop you back to college?' Cathy asked.

Tiffany had received texts from her college dorm mates earlier in the day letting her know that a journalist had been set up outside the college asking other student's their thoughts on Tiffany's case. Not wanting to jump from the frying pan into the fire, Tiffany opted for the safe choice of spending some time at the Jefferson's house before attempting to go home.

As the car pulled up into the driveway, Tiffany saw the hunched figure of Harley pushing a lawnmower across the yard. He stopped for a moment when he registered his mum and Tiffany had arrived home. With a brisk wave and a swipe of his arm across his forehead, he continued to mow.

Tiffany inhaled the scent of the freshly mown grass. The smell reminded her of days when her dad would mow the lawn before they would then head to the beach to frolic in the summer sun.

Tiffany followed Cathy into the kitchen and they sat making small talk while Cathy made them a cup of tea. Eventually, the hum of the mower died down and a few moments later, Harley walked into the kitchen to wash his hands and have a drink of water.

'How did today go?' Harley asked as if it was the most normal thing in the world that Tiffany was sitting in his family's kitchen.

'It was horrible. I was cross-examined for hours. They made everything I said sound like I was an incompetent moron.'

'I know that feeling,' Harley said, making Tiffany feel guilty for all the times in his court case that he had looked uncomfortable and she, in return, had felt pleased.

Cathy interjected, 'Harley, it is a bit different. You were being tried in a criminal case where you had done the wrong thing. Tiffany is being ridiculed in a civil case. She shouldn't have to defend herself when she's done nothing wrong.'

'I wasn't trying to suggest it is the same, just that I know the feeling of being humiliated in front of the court.'

Tiffany felt awkward that Cathy was defending her against her son. 'I think tomorrow they will cross-examine me again and then they will move on with different experts. I'm hoping that by the end of next week, all evidence will be given.'

'So, if you win, are you planning with proceeding with getting pregnant straight away?' Harley asked.

'The embryo is only getting older each day. The sooner it is implanted, the better chance it has of taking. It won't be the oldest embryo ever used, but it won't be far off.'

'So, will the baby call you its mother or sister?' Harley enquired.

'Well, I guess because I will be giving birth to it, I will be its mum, although obviously, we will have the bond of being siblings. I will have to work out how and when to explain it all to the child. *If* there is a child.'

Ruby bounded into the room and nudged her nose against Tiffany's leg. Tiffany leant down and affectionately ruffled the hair on Ruby's head.

'I know there are a lot of people weighing in on the argument over whether you should be allowed to do this, but in my mind, it is cut and dried. You own the embryo so it should be your choice,' Harley said, leaping up to sit upon the kitchen bench.

'Thanks, Harley. Not a lot of people agree with you, but I don't care. I want to do what I feel is right for me.'

Cathy laid her hand over the top of Tiffany's hand. 'We will support you whatever happens.'

'Thank you. It means a lot to me,' Tiffany said, patting Cathy's hand.

The following day, Tiffany took her place on the witness stand once more. Although the day before had been harrowing, Tiffany had made a silent pact with herself to not let the defendant's barrister affect her. She held her head high and answered every question succinctly. After two hours of intensive questioning, she was asked to vacate the witness stand and they called upon Dr Gibson.

When Tiffany had first met Dr Gibson, she felt he was an assertive and bombastic man, yet sitting in the witness box, he seemed a shrivelled and cautious version of himself. Tiffany was glad that she wasn't the only one intimidated by being put on the spot. Phil began his interrogation, asking for Dr Gibson's qualifications, asking about the number of procedures he and the clinic performed each year. He queried whether Dr Gibson remembered Sandra Parker and whether he'd had a specific discussion with her where she had said she didn't want the embryo implanted in Tiffany. Finally, Phil questioned why the clinic did not have a clause in its contract excluding the use of the embryo if it is inherited, if the clinic deemed it unethical.

Dr Gibson stuttered his responses and Tiffany suspected he was feeling the same level of frustration that she had felt the previous day.

Phil finished his assault with the question, 'Isn't the unethical practice here charging someone a sizeable fee every year to keep an embryo frozen if you then refuse to let that person use it?' The barrister for the defendant objected and with a smirk, Phil retracted his question.

The seesawing of questions continued after a short recess, with the defendant's barrister leading Dr Gibson through his affidavit, stating that he was a well-renowned doctor with many years of experience; his opinion that there was a very low probability that the embryo would even be able to be implanted and the fact that the ethics committee had precedence of rejecting a requested implantation where a patient was considered too old, too young or incapable of raising a child, therefore highlighting the fact that there was nothing personal in the rejection of Tiffany's case. The barrister interjected with questions for further clarification. The examination continued for several hours. By the time he left the witness box, Tiffany felt Dr Gibson appeared to be a kind old doctor just looking out for her interests, rather than the objectionable man she had encountered.

Day four of the court case saw Dr Grace Flanders called as a witness. Tiffany's barrister asked questions where Grace calmly offered a professional opinion that Tiffany had dealt well with her grief and mourning. She stated she believed Tiffany was in a sound state of mind to make the decision of whether or not to have the embryo implanted. By the time the defendant's barrister had finished with Dr Flanders, she had exposed that in the records she had made throughout the prior year, she had written she was worried that Tiffany was suffering depression and post-traumatic stress as well as transferred guilt for her parent's death. She also confirmed that Tiffany had been to see her for a professional consultation only a few months prior that led her to diagnose Tiffany with suffering stress. Her subpoenaed files confirmed she had written Tiffany a prescription for sleeping tablets to help her sleep and cope with the stress. The more Dr Flanders gave evidence, the more it appeared to Tiffany that she would be perceived as suffering from mental illness. Unfit to be a parent. Tiffany's stomach was in knots and trying to interpret the judge's opinion made her mind spin.

As the day drew to a close, Tiffany steeled herself for the waiting media circus. She followed Phil outside. After hearing him gasp, Tiffany peeked around from behind him. A picket line of people were carrying posters emblazoned with slogans such as 'Only God makes babies', 'Ban the freeze', 'Unfair for the child' and 'Mother or Sister?'. Tiffany had been aware that Planned Parenthood clinics had suffered attacks from people who believed abortion was an abomination, but she never thought having a child would bring upon her the ire of a group of religious zealots.

As much as reporters calling out her name and asking questions had seemed an invasion of privacy, having people yelling at her that she was a disgrace, that her parents would turn in their graves and that she was just an attention seeker, took her discomfort to a new level.

Phil ushered Tiffany back inside the courthouse and they waited until they could get a police escort. While they waited, Tiffany watched reporters recording their news cross for that night. Tiffany was certain the interest in her case would be at fever pitch after this stunt. She wasn't out to hurt anyone and it troubled her that so many people had ethical concerns with her choice. As she saw it, she was a lonely person, looking to finally give life to her unborn sibling. She thought it should be seen as honourable, not disgraceful. After waiting fifteen minutes, uniformed police cleared a pathway through the protestors and escorted Tiffany to her car. She drove away at record pace, wanting to put distance between her and the milling crowd of parasites feeding off her pain and suffering.

Tiffany sat on her bed, streaming the news live to her laptop. Up until this point, she had avoided watching what the media had to say about her case, but after the flash mob of protestors today, she couldn't help but be curious as to how she was being portrayed.

She was the lead story on the six o'clock news. A close up of her face was in a box on a screen behind the newsreader with a headline *Maybe Baby*. 'The court case of Tiffany Parker versus Gibson Clinic continued to be flanked by controversy today. Parker is suing Gibson Clinic to be given the approval to proceed to have her biological twin implanted in her. This is the first case of its kind where a sibling has requested to give birth to a frozen embryo from their parent. Today, protestors from the Christian Association of Life, who have a history of being anti-frozen reproduction, bombarded Ms Parker. We cross to our reporter on the scene, Ashleigh Carter.'

A slim young woman stood on the steps to Manly Court, holding a chunky microphone in her hand. 'It was utter chaos today for Tiffany Parker. Tiffany's parents died last year, leaving her the heir to their estate. Part of her inheritance was a frozen embryo, a biological twin, conceived at the same time as Tiffany. She is in the process of suing Gibson's Clinic to have her twin implanted in her, making her the first person in the world to do so. Today, a mass of people from the 'Christian Association of Life' rallied out the front of the Manly Courthouse, all chanting slogans highlighting their disapproval of frozen reproduction. I spoke with Mary Ardley, their spokesperson, and this is what she had to say.' The shot changed to a close up of an elderly lady in grey pants and a white blouse. 'Science has a lot to answer for! God made people the way they are so that a man and woman can biologically have a child together. If they can't do that naturally, then that is God's will. What fate will behold this child if it is born to its sister? Next, will we agree that we can give birth to our dog's puppies? How far will we intervene with nature? There is a natural order of events and it is irresponsible to meddle with that. I think what Ms Parker wants to do is a disgrace and an abomination. As much as I don't normally agree with the Gibson's Clinic procedures, I was glad to hear that common sense has prevailed with them seeing the ethical issues associated with this procedure. I hope that this court case opens their eyes to the aberrant actions that they perform daily.'

The screen crossed back to Ashleigh Carter. 'In court today, Ms Parker's psychiatrist gave evidence stating that Ms Parker has a history of suffering depression, PTSD and transference of guilt after her parents' deaths. She then went on to confirm Ms Parker takes sleeping tablets to help her cope with the stress she is under, which left the defence questioning whether she is in a mental state to go through with the procedure and care for a baby. As if today was not stressful enough in court, the surging crowd of picketers outside the courthouse left Ms Parker so distressed this afternoon that she was ushered back inside the confines of the court until she could secure a police guard. Whilst today's protest was considered peaceful, police did warn the crowd that obstructing Ms Parker's freedom again might result in an arrest. This landmark case is being watched intently by reproductive clinics worldwide, as it will set precedence for future cases. In a statement today by Gibson's Clinic, they advised that the terms of their current contracts are being updated to include a clause stating that any patient using their freezing facility will have to provide exact instructions of what they want to happen with any unused eggs upon their death or divorce, otherwise, the embryo will be destroyed. It is hard to believe that they have never included this clause in previous contracts. This case has certainly opened up a can of worms for the industry. We contacted the Minister for Families and Community Services today for a comment, but she declined to issue a statement regarding this case, declaring she doesn't want to interfere with the judicial process. Intrigue in this story continues to grow every day and we will keep you up to date with any developments as they come to hand. Ashleigh Carter, national news.'

Tiffany slammed the screen of her laptop shut and burst into tears. She wasn't sure why her life had turned into a soap opera. She hoped if she won the case that people would leave her alone, but she feared that perhaps the stigma and interest in this ground-breaking case might follow her and the baby for years to come. For the first time in months, she considered whether the stress was all too much and whether she should just drop the case and shrink back into obscurity.

When Tiffany awoke the following morning, she took a look at her puffy red eyes in the mirror and wondered whether there was enough makeup in her kit to conceal the tell-tale signs that she had cried herself to sleep.

A gentle knock on the door startled her. Her heart rate quickened as she worried a reporter had found their way to her dorm room. She tip-toed to the door and looked through the spy-hole. On the other side of the door stood Gabby.

Tiffany opened the door slightly and stuck her head out. 'Hi,' she whispered.

'Hi, Tiff. Can I come in?' Gabby asked quietly.

Tiffany ushered her into her dorm room and locked the door behind them.

'What are you doing here? Aren't you supposed to be in Bathurst for uni?' Tiffany asked.

'I'm here to apologise, Tiff. It's been months since we spoke and so I thought since you won't take my calls, it was best to come and see you face to face. I never meant to hurt you. I just wanted to be honest with you.'

'I know that. I've just been so stressed that I haven't been in the mood to talk to anyone that is against me. I've got enough people that think I'm crazy, without choosing to hang out with them.'

'I don't think you're crazy. I understand why you want to do this,' Gabby said with a timid smile. 'Please forgive me. I've missed you so much.'

Tiffany stepped forward and hugged Gabby, sobbing silently against her shoulder. When she managed to control her crying, Tiffany stepped back to look at Gabby. 'I'm sorry I've been ignoring you. I've really missed you too.'

'Do you remember in fifth grade we made a pinky promise to be BFFs for life? You have to honour that promise, Tiff,' Gabby said, thrusting her pinky finger in the direction of her friend as she had done when they were eleven years old. Tiffany linked her pinky with her friend and they shook their hands vigorously, laughing at the absurdity of their actions.

Gabby released her hand and then reached into her oversized handbag. 'I brought a peace offering.' She delved into the bag and, with a flourish, extracted a boxed Nutella doughnut. 'If you didn't agree to be my friend, I was going to torture you by eating this in front of you!'

Tiffany grabbed the gooey doughnut. 'That would have been unforgiveable.' She laughed as she sunk her teeth into the glazed pastry, letting the choc-hazelnut filling ooze through her mouth, distracted for a moment from her worries by the decadence of eating the delicious treat.

'Okay, I also happen to have my makeup kit with me, so once you finish eating that, have a shower and I will do your makeup. You can't go to court looking like an emotional wreck. If that doughnut hasn't given you a natural glow, my makeup will. You just need to keep your head high, look presentable and professional and then I'm sure the judge will have to award the case to you!'

Tiffany smiled, her teeth coated with dark chocolate filling.

'Oh, and make sure you brush your teeth. It looks like every tooth in your head is rotten,' Gabby said, laughing at her friend.

Once Tiffany was ready to leave, she took one last look at her reflection in the mirror. Staring back at her was the reflection of a confident, almost happy girl. The sugar hit had instantly worked to give her energy and her reconciliation with Gabby gave her a sense of inner peace she had been missing for months. The miracle Gabby had performed with her makeup was astonishing. Tiffany rarely wore more than a swipe of mascara and some lip-gloss. Apart from trying to follow some makeup tutorials on YouTube one lonely Friday night, Tiffany had never managed to use foundation, eyeliner and mascara to give herself a polished appearance. Now, with her mask in place, Tiffany felt ready to forge on with the battle ahead.

Tiffany had lost track of the number of expert witnesses that were being called to give evidence. There was an accountant, a family law expert, an independent psychiatrist, an ethics and philosophy lecturer from a pre-eminent university, a doctor from the medical council, a post-natal care midwife and, finally, a will dispute lawyer.

Today's witness was a chartered accountant, who specialised in investing inheritances. He wore a drab brown suit and his expression matched the dullness of his clothing. For every question he answered in a sense that Tiffany felt supported her case, he would then contradict himself with information that seemed to support the defence. His monotone voice droned on and Tiffany found her attention waning. She thought back to the morning and her relief at having reunited with Gabby. She hadn't told Gabby about her new-found friendship with the Jefferson family. She wasn't really sure how to process their support of her in this time of stress nor did she feel ready to share with her friend that her resentment towards Harley was fading. She had thought that she would hold a grudge against him and his family until her last breath, but their unsolicited warmth and kindness had taken her by surprise, making her question her impressions of them.

Tiffany looked towards the public gallery and saw Cathy sitting quietly in the back corner once again. Her silent support a crutch to prop Tiffany up. Tiffany gave a very timid smile in her direction and Cathy smiled in return while nodding silently. Her simple sign to show Tiffany that she was there for her.

Trying to focus her thoughts on the accountant once more, Tiffany interpreted, amongst the jargon he uttered of investments, yields and growth, that he was of the opinion that the full amount of her inheritance would be enough to support her and a child. In cross-examination, the accountant then confirmed that the average cost of raising a child to the age of 18 is roughly $1 million, if attending private schools. When questioned whether *half* the inheritance would be sufficient for Tiffany to live a comfortable life and raise a child, the drab man stated that he would have concerns that it would stretch that far. Tiffany's shoulders slumped. She scribbled a note to Phil to say that they hadn't taken into account her earning potential. He nodded as he read the note and added it to his ever-increasing pile of loose pages to refer to later in the case.

Day after day, experts were presented to give their professional advice on her life. Dissecting her personal life in front of the media, for the whole world to digest for their entertainment later that night. Each afternoon, she charged through the growing crowd of people. Some were there to see this freak-show first hand but most came to hurl abuse at her. Occasionally, a lone voice could be heard in support of her, but those words were quickly drowned out by the mob.

Finally, after nine excruciating days of evidence, the judge listened to the barristers' final summations. He then advised the court to re-assemble in two weeks for his judgment. Tiffany heaved a sigh of relief. There was no more anyone could do or say. Her destiny lay in the hands of the judge.

Fighting her way through the milling crowds outside the court for the last time for a few weeks, Tiffany spotted Cathy's little white Corolla parked at the curb. She walked to the passenger door to talk to Cathy and thank her for her presence and support. Sitting in the passenger seat was Harley. Cathy had obviously left earlier to pick him up from university and had returned to watch from afar the antics of the pack of media milling around the steps of the courthouse.

'Congratulations, it's almost over now,' Harley said.

Tiffany tried to respond but was distracted by a fluffy boom microphone resting on her shoulder.

Turning around to face the journalist, Tiffany was impatient. 'Can you give me some space?'

'Is that your boyfriend?' the reporter asked. 'Get a photo of the boy,' the journalist directed the cameraman.

'Hop in,' Harley said, keen to be away from the limelight.

Gratefully, Tiffany opened the back door of the car and slid into the sanctuary of the car.

'Thanks for rescuing me again,' Tiffany said.

'That's what we are here for,' Cathy said as she expertly darted out into the traffic, leaving the horde behind.

As Cathy pulled into their suburban street, Harley gasped.

'What's wrong?' Tiffany asked, concerned the media had found where she had headed.

'Oh, it's nothing. It's just that there's a Department of Corrections car parked out the front of our house. They turn up to do random checks to see that I'm complying with my bond conditions. I only have permission to go to and from university, to schools for the education lectures I give and to visit the cemetery once a week. I just hope that I don't get in trouble for having been in Manly with Mum to collect you.'

As they parked in the driveway, the officer walked up to greet them.

'Hello, Harley and Cathy,' a middle-aged man said, shaking Harley's hand.

'Hi,' Harley responded, a guilty look flooded his face.

'Come in, Bill. I'll put the kettle on,' Cathy said, smiling widely, although Tiffany noticed the smile did not reach her eyes.

As they entered the house, Cathy whispered to Tiffany that she should wait in the lounge room.

Feeling guilty for jeopardizing Harley's bond conditions, Tiffany sat quietly trying to eavesdrop on the conversation in the kitchen. The boiling kettle made it hard to make out the whole exchange, but Tiffany sensed the officer was reading Harley the riot act for not being home by an allotted time.

Cathy interjected, 'Bill, I have taken on the responsibility of driving Harley to and from university. Today, I had to deviate to collect his friend, Tiffany, from a court appearance, as she has no one else; but Harley did not leave the car. He cannot be held accountable for the fact that I was driving and I made the decision to drive to Manly. The guilt of this minor misdemeanour lies solely with me. Harley has followed the rules of his home detention to the letter and he shouldn't be blamed for my actions. Please, Bill, you know Harley is a good kid. Can you please see it in your heart to overlook this?'

The kettle whistled loudly, interrupting the conversation.

The scrape of a chair, followed by footsteps and

the kettle silencing, created a void of noise. The clink of mugs being removed from the cupboard the only sound to be heard. Tiffany held her breath, waiting for the officer to speak.

'Given the fact that this is your first minor breach in protocol, I'm willing to not report this incidence, but, Harley, you need to understand that if I find you breaking the terms of your bond once again, you will need to go to court and risk having your home detention revoked and you may be incarcerated instead.'

Tiffany could hear Harley and Cathy simultaneously sigh in relief.

'Thank you. I promise I will only travel to and from university,' Harley said with gravity.

'Thank you so much, Bill. Now, would you like tea or coffee? Cathy asked, her voice chirpy.

'Thanks, Cathy, but I actually have to get going. I have another few house calls to make before I call it a night.'

As they walked towards the front door, Tiffany pulled her phone from her handbag and sat staring at it in an attempt to disguise that she had been eavesdropping on the conversation.

As soon as the officer left the house, Harley joined Tiffany in the lounge room. His face was white and he sighed heavily.

'Is everything okay?' Tiffany asked, feigning ignorance.

'Yep,' Harley said with a tight smile.

Reaching out to touch Harley's arm, Tiffany stared into the depths of his blue eyes, 'I'm really sorry if your mum taking pity on me and coming to check on me today has caused you any problems.'

'It's all fine,' Harley said dismissively.

Tiffany knew Harley had to be feeling rattled. Less than a year shy of his home detention finally being over, the last thing he wanted to do was risk being in breach of his bond conditions and find himself back in court and possibly sent to jail.

'So, do you want a cup of tea or coffee?' Harley said, rising from his seat, Tiffany's hand slipped limply from where it had been resting on his forearm.

'I'd love a tea.' Tiffany rose and followed Harley into the kitchen.

As they entered the kitchen, Tiffany was surprised to find Cathy with her back to them. She stood stock still, like a mannequin in a shop window.

'Mum, do you want a cup of tea?' Harley asked as he re-boiled the kettle.

Cathy was roused from her trance-like state. She turned and hugged Harley fiercely. 'I'm so sorry, Harley. I could have been responsible for you being sent to jail today. I promise I won't jeopardise things for you again. I feel sick when I think of what might have happened if Bill had made a formal

report about you not being here when he arrived.'
She shrank against her son's broad chest and sobbed
quietly.

Harley hugged his mum, patting her back gently;
soothing her, as Tiffany imagined Cathy must have
done to him as a child. 'Shhh, it's okay. There's no
use in thinking about something that didn't happen.
I'm just lucky Bill is a decent guy.'

Tiffany was touched by the obvious deep
connection they shared. A connection she hoped to
emulate one day with her baby.

Cathy took a deep breath and Tiffany watched as
she gained control once more, transforming back
into the capable outgoing mother, the vulnerable
shell of a woman that had just been enveloped in her
son's arms disappeared.

The kettle whistled and Cathy made everyone hot
beverages. Tiffany was reminded of how her mum
used to believe a cup of tea was a remedy for
healing anything.

The three of them sat at the kitchen table in
companionable silence; each reflecting on the
hurdles they had all overcome that day.

The serenity was shattered as Kayla burst
through the front door, 'Yo, yo, yo. I'm home!'

Tiffany watched as Cathy and Harley shared a
smile. Kayla's extroverted enthusiasm for life was
infectious. 'We're in the kitchen,' Cathy called out.

As Kayla entered the kitchen, she didn't even do

a double take at Tiffany's presence. 'Hi, guys. I'm glad you're here, Tiffany. I need to choose an outfit to wear out this weekend. Can you come and have a look at my wardrobe?'

Tiffany's heart swelled. This subtle act had made her feel accepted and part of the family. Here in the warmth of the Jefferson's suburban kitchen, she wasn't treated like the freak that wanted to give birth to her twin, she was just accepted for who she was.

'Kayla, Tiffany has enough on her plate without being your personal stylist,' Cathy remonstrated.

'I'm happy to give you my opinion. I might even have to borrow some of your clothes,' Tiffany replied, a smile lighting up her face.

Later that evening when Martin arrived home, he seemed distracted.

'What's up?' Kayla asked her dad.

'I was listening to the radio on the way home and they were discussing Tiffany's case. They said that Harley was there to pick her up from court today and then the whole discussion turned to his case and his responsibility for killing Tiffany's parents. They had people calling in to have their say on what they were referring to as a freak show. They were questioning Tiffany's sanity, firstly wanting to have this procedure and then asking why she would befriend her parents' killer. It is so wrong that people that have never met these two should be allowed to voice their opinions on what is going on.'

'Don't let it bother you, Dad,' Harley said. 'We've already heard all the horrible things people have to say about me and it hasn't changed who I am. I'm more concerned for Tiffany having to cope with these vultures using her story as entertainment.'

Tiffany nodded. 'I'm stronger than a lot of people think. I've dealt with the worst of it now. In a few weeks, people won't even remember my name.' She smiled with a level of confidence she didn't really feel.

Kayla had been strangely quiet as she scrolled through her phone. 'Guys, you have to hear this. A trashy mag has put this on its online feed. "Woman who wants to give birth to her twin, in love with the man that killed her parents. If you thought this was stranger than fiction, think again. Tiffany Parker is currently suing the Gibson Clinic to allow her to give birth to a frozen embryo that is her biological twin. As court concluded today, she was met by her boyfriend – none other than Harley Jefferson, the man responsible for the accident that killed Tiffany's parents in November 2015. Jefferson was given a good behaviour bond and home detention, but it seemed that wasn't enough to keep him away from supporting his girlfriend. So, the question is, will Jefferson raise his girlfriend's twin as his own child?

'The judgement for the court case, that will determine whether Tiffany can give birth to her twin, is due to be handed down in two weeks. We will keep you posted on any updates as they come to hand." They have a photo of you, Harley, in handcuffs that must have been taken at your trial and a photo of Tiffany mid-blink. You both look like you've escaped from an insane asylum. This is a classic.' Kayla laughed raucously. 'Wow, I didn't know you two were in love and going to raise this baby together. Things have moved really quickly for you.'

'Shut up, Kayla,' Harley said, shaking his head and rolling his eyes.

Tiffany turned to Harley. 'What if the parole board reads that? You might have your bond revoked. It's bad enough that I'm being ridiculed, without your name being dragged through the mud.'

'I don't think anyone with half a brain reads click bait like that. Don't worry about it.'

'Well, I just read it,' Kayla interjected.

'Exactly,' Harley said, laughing. 'Don't be concerned, Tiffany, tomorrow it will all be yesterday's news.'

'I certainly hope you're right, Harley,' Martin said. 'You both have enough stress to deal with, without them making up stories about you.'

CHAPTER 28

Time is a strange thing. When you are impatient, every minute takes forever, but when an essay is due, you blink and a week has gone. Tiffany sat at her desk, completing an assignment that was due the following day. She wanted to lodge it online that night because, in the morning, she knew she would be a bundle of nerves. Tomorrow, the judge would finally hand down his determination and Tiffany struggled to focus her thoughts on anything outside of the court case. She knew that she had only given her assignment a half-hearted effort, but Tiffany placated herself that she was doing the best she could under the circumstances. She only aimed to get a pass for the assignment, quoting Gabby's mantra, *P's get degrees*, over and over in her head. As soon as her fate was known, Tiffany planned on focusing her efforts on studying hard to help get her grade point average up again.

The following morning, Tiffany awoke to the sound of an alert on her phone. She cracked one eye

open and unlocked her phone to see a text from
Gabby.

Sorry I can't be there with you today. Good
luck.

Nervous butterflies jittered in Tiffany's stomach.
She felt a mixture of anxiety and relief that, as of
today, her future would become clearer. She would
either have to accept that she couldn't give birth to
this child or she would need to start planning on
becoming pregnant.

Her phone beeped again, this time a message
from Harley.

*Good luck with the case today. Sorry I can't be
there, but Mum and Kayla will be there to support
you.*

Tiffany felt grateful that the Jefferson family had
taken her under their wings. Although they were
bound by ties that should have made them enemies,
Tiffany felt that strangely enough, the Jefferson's
seemed to be the only ones who had supported her
unconditionally.

Tiffany walked towards the courthouse with Phil
and Mark flanking either side of her. With her head
down, she pushed through the throng of media

waiting outside the courthouse.

When she finally entered the courtroom, Tiffany took a deep breath, breathing in the stale air of the wooden panelled chamber. She hoped this was the last time she would need to see the inside of a courtroom again.

As people filed in, Tiffany was relieved to see her Aunty Jody and Uncle Alex sitting near Cathy and Kayla in the public gallery. Having their silent support bolstered Tiffany's confidence, that regardless of the outcome, she would be able to get through the day.

The court went silent as they all rose for the judge. Once he was seated, the chamber all sat in unison, with bated breath, awaiting the monologue that would settle the case.

Peering over the glasses perched on the end of his nose, the judge looked at both parties.

'In the matter of Ms T Parker vs The Gibson's Clinic, I have heard all evidence and have made a determination based upon all testimonies.

'This case is unique, but in a world of ever-changing familial relationships, I don't wish to dwell on what is considered normal.

'The Gibson's Clinic has raised questions regarding the suitability of Ms Parker as a parent. I believe that other women choosing to have IVF with donor zygotes are not put through this scrutiny; therefore, I discount all evidence in regards to

whether they believe morally, financially or
ethically that she may be unfit.

'There was also doubt cast upon Ms Parker's
mental health, which I find based upon clinical
advice, that she did suffer from a reasonable amount
of depression as she mourned the loss of both her
parents, however, I believe she is now in sound
mind to make a decision of this magnitude.

'In regards to the question as to whether this case
falls into the law governing incest, I rule that as
there is no sexual context, this case does not fall
under this law.

'The crux of the issue raised is really whether the
frozen embryo is considered a person or property.
There is sufficient precedence to determine that the
embryo is, in fact, the property of Ms Parker, having
been inherited by her upon her parents' deaths. As
there were no specific instructions left as to what
David and Sandra Parker wanted to be done with the
embryo, it is within Ms Tiffany Parker's rights to
choose what she wants to do with her property.

'I acknowledge that if the embryo becomes a
child that survives to the age of eighteen, it may
have the right to dispute the distribution of the
Parker's estate, however, the responsibility for
bringing about such a dispute will lie with the said
child.

'Whilst Dr Arthur Gibson is within his rights to
refuse to care for Ms Parker due to his own ethical

conflict, I order that another suitably trained doctor working for the Gibson's Clinic must be made available to perform the IVF procedure to implant the embryo into Ms Parker, if she so desires. There is no reason for this case to be treated any differently than other donor embryo implantations that are done routinely in the Gibson's Clinic.

'I award this case in the favour of Ms Parker, ruling that she must be able to proceed with implantation of the frozen embryo without any restriction and rule that all court costs are the responsibility of the Gibson's Clinic.'

Tiffany's knees were weak. Her pent-up anxiety was relieved and tears of joy ran freely down her face.

Mark thumped her back, 'Congratulations, we did it!' His exuberance was infectious.

'Thank you, Mark. I couldn't have done it without you.'

Turning to Phil, Tiffany put her hand on his. 'Thank you too, Phil. You have put in so much work and effort over the past few months. I know this has been a huge case and you took a big leap of faith in representing me. I know this could have backfired and it would have been so public, so thanks for going out on a limb to help me.'

'I'm so glad the judge awarded the case to you. It has been a tough year for you. You know that you can take your time to decide if you want to proceed with the implantation, this ruling will stand for as long as you own the embryo. It will also be okay if you decide you don't want to proceed. The main thing we wanted was to maintain your right to choose what you want to do.'

Tiffany nodded whilst digesting what Phil had said. It only just dawned on her that while he had obviously wanted to win the high-profile case, he didn't necessarily agree with her having the child.

Looking over towards the defence, Tiffany took in the defeated demeanour of Dr Gibson. He looked smaller and frailer than the belligerent old man she had first met. As he hunched over the desk in discussions with his barrister, Tiffany couldn't help but feel like gloating that this cranky old man hadn't managed to stop her. She made a mental note that it was a good life lesson for her to learn to fight for what you want in life and to not let people stand in your way.

Tiffany walked out of the courtroom into the waiting arms of Cathy and Kayla.

'Congratulations, Hun,' Kayla said. 'I always knew you would win.'

'I'm so happy for you, Tiffany,' Cathy said, a grin lighting up her face.

'So, when are you getting knocked up then?' Kayla asked brashly.

Tiffany laughed, 'I haven't thought that far

ahead. I just wanted to get the ruling today and then make a plan based on the result.'

Jody and Alex joined the group, each hugging Tiffany and offering her their congratulations on the win. When Tiffany introduced Cathy and Kayla to her aunt and uncle, she noticed an element of recognition and even slight disdain for them from Jody. She understood Jody and Alex's reservations about the Jefferson family, as she too had felt the same way about them only a few months prior. To smooth over this, Tiffany told her aunt and uncle about how she had become close to the Jefferson family after Cathy had rescued her several times from the ferocious pack of media. After making small talk, Tiffany noticed the body language of her aunt and uncle change to look more relaxed.

Tiffany looked around the small assembled group and felt overwhelmed with gratitude for her supporters. She knew that while it was still a long road ahead, she had people around her that really cared about her and she appreciated how precious that was. After losing her parents, she would never again take for granted the people in her life.

Phil walked over, and after shaking Alex's hand, he prompted Tiffany to face the crowd of waiting media outside the courthouse. She had decided that she would give a speech to the media in the hope that it would prompt them to leave her alone. The week before, she had written two versions. Today, she was glad that she only had to say the version that proclaimed that she had won.

Phil and Mark stood like sentinels either side of her, while the milling pack of media formed a semi-circle in front of her.

'Today, I was awarded the right to choose what I do with the frozen embryo that I own. Whilst the Gibson's Clinic tried to oppress and intimidate me, I stood up to them. In this case, the defence proceeded to cast aspersions on me and I have had to suffer the constant harassment of the media and those who don't agree with my choice. Today, justice has been served as the Gibson's Clinic was ordered to allow me to proceed with the implantation of the frozen embryo if I so choose. Now that the judgment has been handed down, I can decide what my next step is. I would like to thank my lawyer, barrister, extended family and friends for their support. I ask that now that the case is over, I be given privacy to decide how I wish to proceed. Thank you.'

A barrage of questions was fired at Tiffany, but Phil simply stepped forward and advised that her statement was complete and that she wouldn't be answering any further questions. The media crowd began to thin as they rushed off to lodge their stories, all of them wanting to get the scoop of being the one to release the 'breaking news'. A small group of protestors moved forward, yelling out that Tiffany was 'sick' and 'selfish'. For the last time, Tiffany was ushered through the crowd and was relieved to see Cathy's little white Corolla waiting at the curb in readiness to whisk her away once again.

'So, we've decided that we need to get champagne to celebrate. You've got to have a drink before you're preggers!' Kayla said enthusiastically as they drove towards Roseville.

'That sounds like a great idea,' Tiffany responded, smiling widely.

'I thought, if you don't have any plans, that you might like to stay for dinner tonight. I can make a celebratory meal,' Cathy said.

'Thank you, that would be lovely.'

Tiffany was distracted by a text message from Phil. He had been approached to be interviewed on a current affairs program and had been asked whether Tiffany would be open to discussing her case.

As the car pulled up in the driveway, Harley strode over and opened the door for Tiffany. He wrapped her in his arms, 'Congratulations, Tiff. I'm really happy for you!'

Tiffany returned his hug, feeling comforted by his presence. 'Thanks, Harley.'

'I would have been there if I could have,' Harley

said, 'but at least I had Kayla giving me live updates.'

'I've just received a text message asking me if I am willing to be interviewed for a current's affairs program. What do you think I should do?'

'It's hard to ask for privacy and then do an interview on national TV,' Harley replied.

'How much money will they pay you? You could become rich and famous, Tiff,' Kayla said. 'I've got the perfect outfit for you to wear!'

As they walked inside, Ruby enthusiastically jumped up and down at Tiffany's feet until Tiffany relented and picked her up for a cuddle. Tiffany laughed. 'No, I think Harley is right. The last thing I want is a higher profile because of this. I think Phil is considering doing an interview, so I'm happy for him to take the spotlight.'

'Fair enough. Plus, it's time for you to let your hair down and celebrate with us. I'll just go find some champagne flutes,' Kayla said.

Harley walked towards Tiffany with a bouquet of flowers in a vase. 'These are for you. I couldn't go out to buy you flowers, but I did the best I could to scrounge up some flowers from the garden.'

Tiffany's heart melted. 'Thanks, Harley, that's so kind of you. They mean so much more to me than a bunch from a grocery store. I think it is amazing how you keep the gardens here looking so great.'

Harley's face reddened as he shrugged his

shoulders. 'Yeah, well I have to do something with all my free time.'

Kayla returned with glasses. As she placed them on the kitchen table, she looked at the flowers. 'Are these for me from a secret admirer?'

Harley laughed, 'They're just a small bunch of flowers to congratulate Tiffany.'

'You're one smooth operator, Harley Jefferson,' Kayla teased.

'Shut up and pop the champagne,' Harley responded while rolling his eyes.

With tall, slim champagne flutes fizzing with light bubbles, the Jefferson family toasted Tiffany. As she softly clinked glasses with her new substitute family, Tiffany felt happier than she had in years. Her destiny was now in her hands and she no longer felt isolated and alone.

CHAPTER 29

With her heart racing, Tiffany nervously dialled the Gibson's Clinic to make an appointment with Dr Alison Galway, the female doctor who had quietly supported her cause. Whilst the last few months' focus had been on winning the right to have the embryo implanted, Tiffany still didn't even know whether she was fertile.

The first step was to determine her level of fertility. Being nineteen, Tiffany assumed she would be highly fertile, but she was secretly worried that there may be a genetic reason that she wasn't able to have a child, just as her mum had struggled with her fertility for years. Tiffany knew that it wasn't until you wanted to have a child that you could determine whether you were physically able.

Cathy accompanied Tiffany to her appointment. Having her calm maternal presence helped soothe Tiffany's nerves. She had expected to be greeted hostilely, but the receptionist treated her no differently to the other women waiting for their appointments. Tiffany heard quiet whispers amongst some of the other patients and knew instantly that they were talking about her, but having faced people yelling at her outside court, she knew she could easily cope with hushed whispers. Cathy picked up a tattered old magazine and began to flick through it.

Dr Galway ushered Tiffany into her room and explained the process to her. Today, they would map her menstrual cycle, take blood samples to check her hormone levels, perform tests to rule out any STDs and, finally, do an ultrasound to check that there were no abnormalities in her uterus. If there were a problem with fertility, then hormone injections would be given to boost Tiffany's fertility. If everything was considered normal, then they would plan a date that was optimal for implantation, approximately two weeks after the first day of her period. On that day, Tiffany would be prepped for the procedure. The embryo would then be defrosted and if deemed viable, it would then be implanted. Within two weeks post procedure, they would be able to determine whether the embryo had taken. Tiffany would have to rest to ensure the best possible chance of the embryo attaching. She would be considered high-risk and have regular pre-natal check-ups and then, within nine months, the baby would be born.

It was a lot of information for Tiffany to digest,

so she focused on the procedures for today. Within half an hour, all tests had been completed and Dr Galway assured Tiffany that she would contact her with the results as soon as they were available.

As Tiffany and Cathy walked towards the car, Cathy turned to Tiffany. 'How did things go?' Cathy asked.

'It went well. I should find out in a few days if I'm fertile. I could have the embryo implanted as soon as next month.'

'Wow. It's so exciting. I'm sure you will make an amazing mum.' Cathy covered her mouth. 'Was that wrong to call you its mum? Do you see your relationship as being its mother or its sister? What do you want the child to call you?'

Tiffany hadn't thought about the logistics of what the baby would call her. Having listened to the testimony of the psychiatrist during the trial, she was worried that the child may have problems with self-esteem if it was in a situation so different to the norm. 'I guess I will be its mum. I will be giving birth to it and it won't have its biological parents around.'

Tiffany stopped and looked at Cathy. 'Actually, Cathy, this baby also won't have any grandparents. It does worry me that it will be missing out on so many normal family structures. I've taken to thinking of you like my substitute mum. Would you like to be my baby's Nanna too?'

'I'd be delighted, Tiffany. That is sweet of you to ask. Heaven knows when my own kids will actually settle down and have kids.' Cathy hugged Tiffany, their bond growing stronger every day.

'I have another surprise for you,' Tiffany said, a smile playing on her lips.

Cathy smiled, looking intrigued by the surprise.

'I have arranged for you to have a facial at my mum's favourite day spa, to say thank you for all your support.'

'You don't need to do that. I'm just trying to help fill the void left after the loss of your mum.'

'Cathy, you spend all your time looking after other people. Please go and have some time out for yourself for a change.'

'It is very sweet of you, Tiffany, but I have to pick up Harley from university at 2pm.'

'I will get him from uni. Please, Cathy, it would mean the world to me for you to get pampered for a few hours. Plus, I've already paid for it, so you have to go,' Tiffany said forcefully.

Cathy put her hands up in surrender. 'Okay, thank you, Tiffany. That would be lovely.'

At 2pm, Tiffany sat in her car listening to music as she waited for Harley to finish at a lecture. She had texted him to let him know that she was picking him up, but he hadn't replied, so she was worried that his phone was dead.

She got out of her car so that she could better see all the people milling around. Tiffany could make out Harley's broad shoulders as he walked in the distance. He looked more carefree than she had seen him before. A slender brunette girl walked beside him, laughing and casually touching his arm. Tiffany waved to get Harley's attention. When he raised his hand to wave at her, she slid back into the driver's seat. Watching from the confines of her car, she tried to interpret Harley and the girl's relationship as the girl with the glossy dark hair hugged Harley goodbye.

Sliding into the passenger seat, Harley turned to Tiffany. 'Are you my chauffeur today?'

'Yes, I sent you a text. Didn't you get it?'

'Oh, I forgot my phone today. I think I left it on charge. Where's Mum?'

'I sent her to a day spa to get pampered. She is such a special person and I wanted to thank her for treating me so well.'

'Mum wouldn't expect that. You know it kills me that she has taken on the guilt of my actions. It's like she's made it her mission to make up to you the fact that I was responsible for killing your parents. It's as if she thinks that if she tries hard enough, it will all go away. But it never will.' Tiffany looked at the melancholic look on Harley's face and couldn't help but compare it to the light-hearted look he'd had on his face when he was walking with his friend.

'So, who is the girl you were walking with? She's pretty.'

'Her name's Emily. We have a group assignment and she is in my group. We were just having a laugh at what one of the other group members suggested we do for the assignment.'

'She looks a bit like Tia,' Tiffany said, probing to see if he was attracted to Emily in the way he had been with his girlfriend.

'She's nothing like Tia,' Harley said with a huff.

Tiffany was worried that she had opened old wounds. Instead of seeing the carefree version of Harley, she had only succeeded in bringing about sorrow that hung over them like a fog. Harley's shoulders slumped and he stared out the window.

'Do you miss Tia?'

'Tia was the life of the party. She was so fun to be around. I miss her laugh. It was infectious – even if you weren't in the mood to laugh, within a few seconds of hearing her, you couldn't help but let a smile creep onto your face. She used to do this funny snort thing when she thought something was really hilarious.' Harley had a faraway look in his eyes with a small smile playing on his lips as he reminisced.

'Did you love her?'

Harley sat quietly and his smile faded. Tiffany knew it was hard for him to discuss his feelings, particularly about anything related to the accident and the resulting deaths.

'I really liked Tia, but to be honest, I don't think I could say I loved her. We'd only been dating for a few weeks. Love seems like too heavy a word to describe our relationship. It was just about going out and having fun. I certainly wasn't thinking about wanting to settle down with her or anything.' Harley looked wretched. 'You know the only small amount of peace I can get about the accident, is the fact that Tia was passed out in the passenger seat after she'd had a few too many drinks at the party, which was why I was driving her home. At least she never felt the terror before the impact. They say she died instantly.' Harley's fists were clenched as he talked about the incident. Taking a deep breath, Harley looked out the window again. 'Can we change the subject?'

'I was thinking we could go to the cemetery. I haven't been to visit my parents' graves for a while. Do you feel up to that, or would you rather go home?'

'I don't mind. If you want to go to the cemetery, I'll come,' Harley said, drowning in his guilt.

Silently, Tiffany drove to the cemetery. When they arrived, she turned to walk towards her parents' graves.

'Do you want some time alone?' Harley asked

sullenly. His arms crossed against his chest.

Under normal circumstances, she would have craved solitary time with her parents, but seeing Harley with the weight of the world on his shoulders, Tiffany didn't want to leave him alone with his thoughts.

'No, walk with me,' Tiffany said.

Harley walked beside her with his hands jammed into his pockets and his head down.

'Harley, you can't change the past. Believe me, I wish there was a way, but there isn't. Don't you think that if I can accept that your choices that night were just a huge mistake, then you have to start accepting it too? You're a good guy and it breaks my heart to see you so cut up.'

Harley turned his head away in a weak attempt to disguise his tears.

Tiffany instinctively hugged him, squeezing him as if to transfer her strength to him. Tiffany had never seen Harley submit to his grief and allow himself to show his vulnerability. He wrapped his arms around her, his head resting on hers. Tiffany felt the silent sobs racking his body and she hoped this moment would prove cathartic for him.

When Harley finally pulled away from their embrace, he looked embarrassed. 'I'm sorry to have a break down in front of you. You're the one that has lost more than me.'

'Yes, I've lost my parents. But you have the

burden of guilt for their and Tia's deaths. No amount of berating yourself is going to change what happened. Harley, look at me.' Tiffany positioned herself in front of Harley so she could look directly into his eyes. 'I forgive you.'

Harley's hands tenderly cupped Tiffany's face and he lent down and gently kissed her lips.

Tiffany was surprised by his response, but given the circumstances, she felt he had just been caught up in the emotion of the moment.

When Harley pulled back, his eyes were brimming with tears once more. 'I don't deserve your forgiveness, but thank you.'

'Harley, you need to forgive yourself. It's stupid what ramifications one reckless moment can have on the rest of your life. You are paying the price for your mistake with your loss of independence, but this time next year, you will be free to live your life. You are so lucky that you didn't get killed in the accident too. Don't waste the life that was spared by being fixated on the lives that were lost.'

'I don't understand how you can be so forgiving.'

'I used to want to see you rot in jail, but what would that have achieved? You're in your own private hell now. Did you know I considered dropping my law degree all together as I was so disillusioned with the legal system? I thought you got off scot-free but I now recognise that they got your sentence right. Since I've gotten to know you, I realise that you're a good person with an amazing family. I don't want to see you throw your life away, beating yourself up over what happened. You have an incredible life ahead of you and it would be such a waste not to live it to the fullest.'

'Thank you for believing in me.'

Tiffany grabbed Harley's hand. 'Come on, let's go visit my parents.'

Standing by her parents' graves, Tiffany began to have a conversation with them. 'So, Mum and Dad, you might recognise this guy. He sometimes loiters around here and brings you flowers, but I haven't formally introduced you. This is Harley and he is a really kind, considerate, nice guy. His driving sucks, that's why I drove here today.' Tiffany grinned at Harley. 'He comes from a great family. He has a bold, funny sister and the sweetest mum. She came with me today when I had a doctor's appointment. You see, I won the court case and I can now have the frozen embryo you saved implanted in me. They did tests today to check on my fertility and in a few days, I will know if I can have the embryo implanted next month.'

Harley looked at Tiffany. 'Are you really going ahead with this next month?'

Tiffany grimaced. 'I think so. It depends on the results.'

'Oh my god, Tiff, this is huge.'

'I know, but I wouldn't have fought so hard if I didn't want this so badly.'

Tiffany turned to address the headstones. 'Anyway, Mum, I hope you don't mind, but I've basically adopted Cathy as a second mum and I asked her today if she will be this baby's Nanna. It's really important to me that this child is embraced and loved. I know the birth of this child will be controversial, but I have to ensure it feels wanted and loved.'

'Umm, Mr and Mrs Parker,' Harley interrupted.

'Call them Sandy and Dave,' Tiffany said.

'So, Sandy and Dave, I want you to know that I will look out for Tiffany and this child. We will treat them like family so they know that they are undoubtedly wanted and loved.'

'Awww,' Tiffany said, squeezing Harley's hand. 'Anyway, we have to go now. I have to get this felon back home before he gets thrown into jail.' Tiffany teased. 'I love you, Mum and Dad. Next time I visit, I might be carrying your baby.'

CHAPTER 30

Sitting at her desk, studying for her end of year final exams, Tiffany stared out the window at a small finch sitting on her windowsill. Ever since she had seriously considered the possibility that she may soon be a mother, Tiffany had become increasingly clucky. Any little innocent creature made her heart swell. The vibrating of her phone brought her out of her reverie.

'Hello, Tiffany.'

Tiffany took a deep breath. She had been waiting on this call for days and now she would finally know if she could proceed with implantation.

'Hi, Dr Galway,' Tiffany said. Her eagerness making her voice sound high and squeaky in her own ears.

'I have your results back. Everything seems perfectly normal. Based upon this, I have to ask whether you want to proceed with implantation next month?'

'Yes. I'm ready to go ahead with this.'

'Okay. You need to let me know the day you get

your next period, then twelve days after that, we will schedule an appointment for the implantation. I need to warn you that the embryo is one of the oldest specimens ever used. There is a high chance that it may not be viable. I just want you to be realistic about the slim probability that this will result in pregnancy.'

'I understand. Thank you, Dr Galway.'

'Okay, well you contact me when you get your periods. I'll speak to you then.'

'Thanks, bye.'

As soon as she hung up the phone, Tiffany rang Cathy. 'I just heard from the doctor that everything is okay to proceed in about three weeks.'

'That's great news, Tiffany. I would like you to come and stay at our place after the procedure so you can rest. We want to give this baby the best chance possible.'

'Thanks, Cathy. That would be great. Do you think you would be able to be there as my support person when they do the implant?'

'I'd love to. You just let me know the time and the place.'

'Okay. By the way, can you let Martin, Kayla and Harley know the news.'

'I will.'

'Okay, well, I need to get back to studying. I'll talk to you again soon.'

'Bye, Darling,' Cathy said before hanging up.

Tiffany sent a text message to Gabby.

Looks like I might be pregnant in three weeks. I'll keep you posted.

Although they had reconciled, Tiffany didn't feel as close to Gabby as she had previously and was aware that while Gabby was being supportive, she didn't really agree with Tiffany's choice to have the baby. Within a minute, Gabby had replied to the message:

I'm just heading to an exam. I'll call you tonight. Accompanying the text was a love heart emoji and an emoji of a baby.

Tiffany really needed to focus on studying, but knew she really needed to share her news with her Aunty Jody. She called and Jody answered on the third ring. 'Hi, Sweetheart. How are you?'

'I'm good. I just heard from the doctor and she said I'm fine to get the embryo implanted in about three weeks.'

There was a moment of silence as Jody digested the information. 'Congratulations. I guess this is what you've wanted for a while now. It will be interesting to see if the baby looks just like you.'

'I know you feel about weird about me having this baby, but I couldn't have destroyed it or given it away. You get to have another niece,' Tiffany said brightly.

'It will be weird to see Sandy's baby, but I really only worry about the burden this is going to put on you at such a young age. You have had such a stressful few years. I would like you to be able to be young and carefree, but at the end of the day, it's your life to live.'

'Thanks for your concern, but this is what I want more than anything.'

'Well then, I hope it all goes well.'

'Thanks, Aunty Jody. I have my exams starting tomorrow so I need to go study but I just wanted to fill you in.'

'Thanks, Tiff. Good luck with it all.'

Tiffany stared at the pages of her notes, the words swimming and blurring as her mind was engrossed with cots, prams and baby clothes. She rose and grabbed a pillow from her bed. Stuffing it under her top, she looked at her reflection in the bathroom mirror and marvelled at how bizarre it was that this time the following month she might be pregnant. She seesawed between hoping it was a little girl like her, so that she could share the same bond she had with her mother, then hoping it would be a boy – the son her parents never had.

After half an hour of distractions, Tiffany scolded herself for her lack of discipline and sat at her desk once more. As she studied, she instinctively stroked her stomach.

On the day of her last exam, Tiffany saw the first sign of her periods. This phenomenon was usually met with annoyance, but this time, Tiffany was delighted. She looked forward in her diary to twelve days ahead and marked it as the day for implantation. After a brief phone call to make arrangements with Dr Galway, Tiffany headed off to her exam. She would usually be anxious before an exam, but the timing of her last exam and the fact that she would be finished university for the year just in time to have the embryo implanted made her feel like everything was falling smoothly into place.

Tiffany passed Sunani in the foyer of her college. 'How are your exams going?'

'I just finished my last exam,' Sunani said. 'How about you?'

'Same. I'm done for the year. It feels so liberating.'

'There's a group of us going for drinks tonight. Do you want to join us? I've hardly seen you over the past few months.'

'It has been such a crazy year. I'd love to meet you guys for drinks.'

'So, what's happening with the whole baby thing? I heard you won the court case. Thank god that's over. I got sick of dodging reporters outside. I was starting to feel like Beyoncé.' Sunani laughed.

'Well, between you and me, I'm actually having the embryo implanted in twelve days' time. Hopefully, the media doesn't get wind of that because the last thing I want is to face harassment from the public again.'

'So, you are going to have a baby next year. That's bizarre. I struggle to look after myself, let alone taking on the responsibility of looking after an innocent little baby. Where are you going to live?'

'I don't know yet. If the implant is successful, I will have to give notice here and find a little townhouse nearby.'

'So, tonight will have to be a double celebration.'

'Yes, I guess so. I've got to live it up while I can.'

CHAPTER 31

On the morning of the procedure, Tiffany was up and dressed an hour before she needed to leave. She had packed a small duffle bag of clothes to take to the Jefferson's so she could stay there and rest for a few days.

When Cathy arrived, Tiffany was a nervous wreck.

'What if the embryo disintegrates when they defrost it?' Tiffany voiced her fears aloud for the first time.

'You have no control over that. Let's just think positively that everything will be fine,' Cathy said reassuringly.

'What if Dr Gibson interferes with the embryo so it's not viable?'

'I trust Dr Galway would not let her professional oath to look after you be sabotaged,' Cathy answered calmly.

'What if the media has been tipped off and I have protestors and media waiting there?' Tiffany said, her voice getting more panicked with each scenario.

'Tiffany, take a deep breath. You are a strong, independent woman. You have dealt with worse things than what is going to happen today. You need to just relax and put your trust in the process. If it is meant to be, it will be.'

Tiffany breathed deeply through her nose and held it for six seconds, a technique she had been taught by Dr Flanders to help calm her when she was anxious.

As they pulled into the car park, Tiffany's right leg jiggled nervously.

Cathy put her hand on Tiffany's leg. 'Calm down. You are young and healthy. If this was ever going to work, you are the perfect candidate.'

'Thanks for being here,' Tiffany said. If she couldn't have her mum by her side, Cathy was the next best substitute.

Tiffany lay in a sterile blue hospital gown, upon a cold vinyl padded bed. The stainless-steel stirrups at the end of the bed looked ominous. Cathy stood by Tiffany's side holding her hand.

Dr Galway came into the room, looking calm and confident. 'I have good news. The embryo has been defrosted and it is still viable. It is a miracle that it has endured being frozen for over twenty years.'

'That's a relief,' Tiffany said, smiling at Dr Galway.

'I just need to confirm one final time that you

want me to proceed?'

'Yes,' Tiffany said, her heart racing with nerves. She squeezed Cathy's hand.

Within a few minutes, the procedure was complete.

'Rest and look after yourself. Take things easy for the next two weeks. After that, you can resume gentle exercise.'

'Okay. Fingers crossed that it works,' Tiffany said excitedly.

'I will see you in three weeks if you haven't started your period, at which time I will be able to do a test to confirm whether you are pregnant.'

'Thank you for all your help, Dr Galway,' Tiffany said earnestly. 'I really couldn't have done it without you.'

Cathy had made up the guest bed with soft linen that smelt like a fresh spring day and Harley had placed a bouquet of hand-picked flowers on the bedside table. Tiffany felt embarrassed by the attention the Jefferson's were paying her, like she was an old sick aunt, not a young healthy girl that may or may not be pregnant.

Only Kayla didn't treat her with kid gloves. When she arrived home, she plonked herself down on the bed, next to the spot that Ruby had already claimed when Tiffany had first arrived. 'Tell me all the juicy details, Little Momma.'

Tiffany laughed at Kayla. 'You really don't want to know,' Tiffany said obtusely.

'Okay. Then tell me the one thing you miss the most about your parents.'

Tiffany was thrown off guard. She hadn't expected Kayla to ask her such a personal question. 'You know, my parents used to squash me in a hug between them. They called it a 'Tiffany Sandwich' and I used to think it was so embarrassing, but squished between the two of them was the safest and most loved I have ever felt in my life.'

Rather than delve further into Tiffany's memories, Kayla changed the conversation. 'Speaking of love, there's a guy at uni who is really cute. I don't know if he is keen on me. He asked me to go to a club with him this weekend, but I found out there is a group of people going. What do you think?'

'I don't know. I'm the wrong person to ask. I haven't dated a guy in years.'

'True. Only someone lonely and desperate gets knocked up with their frozen sibling,' Kayla jibed.

Harley walked in with a boxed game of Scrabble. 'Do you want to play?'

'That sounds like fun,' Tiffany said, grateful for a distraction.

'Oh my god. I can't believe I just asked dating advice from a girl keen to play Scrabble. Seriously, you two belong in a retirement village.'

'Why don't you join us, Kayla? It might be fun,' Tiffany said.

'I'd rather kill myself. Plus, I'm starving. Do you want anything from the kitchen?'

'No thanks,' Tiffany said, touched by her offer.

'I'd love some toast,' Harley said, smiling.

'Last time I checked, your legs worked fine, Bro. So, unless you're pregnant with your frozen twin, you can get food for yourself.' Kayla swept out of the room.

Harley and Tiffany laughed at Kayla's comments. Tiffany loved the banter between the brother and sister.

Harley sat on the bed with his leg sporting the electronic monitoring cuff tucked under his body. Tiffany had noticed his embarrassment of the black band that he continually tried to hide from view.

With the board between them, Harley and Tiffany balanced their letter racks on the bed. They were both fiercely competitive and took their time in calculating the highest point scoring word they could. Tiffany was edging ahead, feeling smug that she had the game won, when down to the final letters, Harley placed an X on a triple letter square, just scraping in a win.

'Congratulations,' Tiffany said graciously, shaking Harley's hand.

'Do you want another game?' Harley asked.

'My brain is hurting. Can we just watch TV for a bit?'

'Aren't you bed bound?' Harley asked with concern.

'I'm sure it will be okay to sit on the lounge.'

Tiffany walked gently down to the lounge room. After sitting at the other end of the lounge, Harley gently lifted Tiffany's feet into his lap and began to massage the soles of her feet. 'Why did you get this butterfly tatt on your ankle?'

Tiffany looked at the tiny blue butterfly. 'My mum loved butterflies. I also thought it was symbolic as you know how butterflies start out as caterpillars and then go through metamorphosis to become a butterfly. I thought it was like how I was going to have to reinvent myself after my parents died.'

'That's cool. What about the moon on your wrist?'

'Oh, that's there because my dad used to read a book to me about a rabbit loving its kid to the moon and back.'

'We have that book here somewhere. When I was a kid, my mum used to read it to me every night. I even had a plush toy rabbit that looked like the illustrations in the book.'

'Do you still sleep with it?' Tiffany jibed.

'Every night,' Harley replied sarcastically.

As they watched a mind-numbing reality show on renovating, Harley continued to rub the soles of Tiffany's feet.

'I could get used to this,' Tiffany said, wiggling her toes.

'I promised your parents I'd look after you,' Harley said. He then started wiggling each toe, reciting the children's rhyme, 'this little piggy went to market.' By the time he finished the rhyme, he was madly tickling the sole of Tiffany's foot, making her squirm. She was relieved to see the lighter side to Harley. He seemed to be less morose since their emotional and frank conversation at the cemetery. She enjoyed her time with Harley and had ruminated over the kiss they had shared that day, wondering if it was a spur of the moment thing, or whether it might develop into something. Part of her longed to be with him, while another part debated how wise it would be to get into a relationship with him, as she would risk losing the only version of a family she had if things didn't work out. She decided it was better to stay in the friend zone for the stakes were too high.

The days dragged out, being confined to bed and resting in the lounge room. Thankfully, Tiffany didn't have a lot of time to focus on the possible pregnancy as Harley was always by her side. Being on house arrest, he didn't have a choice to go out, so he was her constant companion. They had played every board game in the house and binge-watched multiple Netflix series. Rather than growing weary of each other, their bond grew tighter - each of them a welcome distraction in the other's life.

'So, Harley, tell me what was running through your head that night when I assaulted you at the toga party,' Tiffany said, cringing at the memory.

'I'd had a few drinks. I thought I was definitely going to be sent to prison and my friends had convinced me that I needed to get out and party before I got locked in the slammer. To be honest, I just wanted a night off, to ignore the guilt that was overwhelming me. Obviously, I didn't recognise who you were. I just thought you were some pretty girl coming up to have a chat with me. As soon as it became clear who you were, I felt like a dick. I knew that it looked bad that I was out partying and not home crying in my pillow. I deserved your anger. You should have punched me in the face, not just shoved me in the chest.'

'It was still all so raw for me. I thought you were this arrogant dude who didn't care about what you had done. I couldn't believe you were out at a party like you didn't have a care in the world. Now I know that wasn't the case, but at the time, I just wanted to see you locked up behind bars. I'm glad now that you didn't get sent to jail.'

'Do you remember I was in prison while we

waited for sentencing? That was the longest two weeks of my life. It is such a cold, institutionalized place. I was so scared that I was going to spend years in jail. I can't tell you how relieved I was when I was told that I could have a good behaviour bond and home detention.'

Tiffany could tell Harley's mood was deteriorating and although she appreciated the heartfelt conversation, she didn't want him to slip into feeling melancholy. 'How about we play Monopoly? That way, we might both be sent to jail.'

'Okay, but take it easy on me this time. You bankrupted me last time we played.'

'So, I did the maths,' Harley said one day as they sat on the lounge. 'I will be able to drive again just before the baby is due. I can drive you to hospital when you go into labour. I can even be your support person if you like.'

'Aww thanks, Harley. I have to wait to see if I'm pregnant first,' Tiffany said.

'Have you had any strange cravings?' Harley asked, as if this was a reliable way to determine pregnancy.

Tiffany laughed, 'You mean like pickles and ice-cream?'

'Yum, I love pickles,' Harley said.

'Maybe you're pregnant,' Tiffany said laughing.

'So, when will you know if you are pregnant?'

Harley asked.

'I have an appointment next week that should confirm it one way or the other.'

'Are you scared?' Harley asked quietly.

'A little bit. I'm also a little bit excited and a little bit worried. It's going to change my life.'

'You'll be a great Mum,' Harley said, patting her leg. 'So, have you considered any names yet?'

'I don't want to get ahead of myself, but I was thinking of incorporating my parents' names if I can. Every time I think about this baby, I just get so excited. I have to keep reminding myself that maybe it won't work but I want to keep a positive mind. It's been great having you to distract me from thinking about this 24/7. If I'd been at home on my own, I would have researched all the things that can go wrong in pregnancy.'

Cathy entered the darkened room. 'You guys know it is a beautiful sunny day outside. Why don't you go and sit on the back lawn for a bit? It will be a nice change of scenery for you.'

'Shall we?' Tiffany asked Harley.

'After you,' he responded.

As they sat in the glaring sun, Tiffany breathed in the scent from the flowers in the garden. Next to her, a fragrant gardenia was in bloom, its petite white flowers rested in the dark green foliage like stars against a night sky. She closed her eyes and let the tranquillity sweep over her. When she opened her eyes, she found Harley staring at her. 'You look so serene.'

Tiffany felt warmth flood her face.

'Have you considered where you are going to live when you leave the college dorms? Maybe you could move in here?' Harley offered.

'I'm sure I have already outlived my welcome. I'm going to move back home in a day or so.' Tiffany looked at the sadness that washed over Harley's face and realised he would be lonely stuck at home on his own again. 'Don't look so glum; I'll still come to visit you. To be honest, you are the only person in the world that I want to beat at cheesy board games.'

Harley scoffed, 'You wish you could beat me. I'm the official Scrabble king.'

'Maybe, but I'm the Monopoly queen.'

Tiffany looked around the yard, still as orderly and well maintained as the first day she saw it. 'Show me what you have planted in this garden.'

Harley stood up and walked proudly to a garden bed planted with azaleas and daisies. 'This was the first garden I did after I was put on home detention. I thought it would be nice to make a pretty floral garden as a thank you to my mum for all her devotion to me. I found it hard to tell her I appreciated that, by agreeing to be my 'carer', she was literally putting herself on home detention too.'

'It's beautiful. You are so lucky to have such a caring family. They really have your back. They've even been amazingly kind to me and I'm not even family.'

'You're an honorary member of our family,' Harley said while draping his arm around her shoulders.

They walked to the opposite side of the yard. 'This garden is like a little tropical oasis. I made this one for Kayla because she always says she would like to live on a deserted island. I couldn't give her the island, but I tried to make the garden resemble a tropical resort.'

'It's gorgeous.'

'And this garden over here is my Zen garden.' Harley led Tiffany behind a hedge to a small area with Japanese plants and carefully raked pebbles in a wavy pattern.

'I never knew this area existed. It's incredible.'

'It is my quiet area for thinking about life. My psychiatrist suggested I meditate to help alleviate the anxiety that builds up some days when I reflect on what happened. I thought I would make a suitable area to escape to, where I can feel calm and in control.'

'You're so talented, Harley. Maybe your skills will be wasted on teaching. Maybe you should become a landscape designer.'

'I enjoy this but I really want to help make a

difference in kids' lives. Having a strong support system for kids can make the difference between them going off the rails or not. I often imagine what my life would have been like if my parents hadn't been so supportive.'

Tiffany reflected on the love and encouragement her parents had always given her and knew that she understood how important it was for kids to feel safe and cared for. She wanted to make sure that this baby would be able to feel secure too.

CHAPTER 32

Tiffany ate her dinner quietly, listening to the rabble of voices around the table. She was going to miss the ordered chaos of living with the Jefferson family.

'Guys, I just wanted to thank you all for allowing me to stay here with you. I've had such a lovely time. I'm planning on heading back to my place tomorrow.'

'That sucks. Can't you stay longer?' Kayla asked, her mouth half full of food.

'I've stayed longer than I should have. You guys must want to get back into your normal routine, without having me here as a freeloader.'

'You are welcome to stay as long as you like,' Cathy said.

'Yeah, Mum has enjoyed having you babysit Harley, so she doesn't have to,' Kayla said, laughing.

'Give her a break. Maybe Tiffany wants some peace and quiet for a change,' Harley replied.

'I have loved being here, but early next week I

will find out what is happening with the baby and I have to start making plans for my future.'

'Well, you're welcome here anytime, Sweetheart,' Cathy said, patting Tiffany's hand.

Changing the topic, Harley declared to the table, 'I think we should have a farewell game of Trivial Pursuit after dinner to mark the occasion.'

'Sorry, I'm cleaning out my sock drawer. I won't be able to join in,' Kayla said.

'Mum and Dad?' Harley pleaded.

'Okay,' they said in unison.

Once the dinner table was cleared, Martin brought in the game of Trivial Pursuit and began setting up the board.

Tiffany excused herself to use the bathroom. She returned a few minutes later, her face white and her eyes glassed over. She walked to Cathy and quietly whispered in her ear.

Cathy's face dropped and she wrapped Tiffany in a hug. Cathy rubbed Tiffany's back.

Martin and Harley looked at the women, then at each other uneasily.

'What's wrong?' Harley asked.

Tiffany extricated herself from Cathy's arms. 'I've got my period,' she said, her bottom lip wobbling.

'Oh, Tiff, I'm so sorry. To think of how hard you fought to have this baby, it seems so unfair.'

Harley got up and hugged Tiffany. His strong arms around her were her undoing and she let herself weep at her loss.

Cathy and Martin quietly exited the room, leaving Tiffany and Harley alone to talk.

'I did everything I could to make this work. I just wanted to have my own family. Living here has shown me how special it is to be surrounded by family. I wanted so badly to give life to the baby that my parents had saved for twenty years. I wanted to look after it and raise it in their honour. The thought of this child gave me hope that I didn't have to be alone anymore. Now, I'm totally on my own.'

'You're not alone. You've got my family and me. I meant it yesterday when I told you that we think of you as an honorary member of our family. I still think you will be an amazing mum one day, but it will just have to be your biological child instead of your parents'. I don't think you could have done anything more to allow this embryo to take. You were told that there was only about a 20% chance it would be successful, that means that there was an 80% chance it wouldn't work.'

'I know, but I put myself through so much public ridicule and fought it in court, just to be allowed to proceed. As soon as you commit to having an embryo implanted, it is hard not to think of it as your baby. As much as I've been trying not to plan too far ahead, I had already worked out its due date and had been thinking about a short-list of names. I feel so stupid for getting carried away when I knew the odds were against me.'

'It's not stupid. You were just thinking positively.'

'I guess Dr Gibson and the protestors from the Christian Association for Life will be grateful that it didn't work out,' Tiffany said bitterly. 'Oh well, at least there won't be a child that suffers mental anguish over its dysfunctional birth. Maybe it is for the best. Maybe it was just a band-aid solution to help alleviate my loneliness.'

Harley stood in front of Tiffany, just as she had with him at the cemetery weeks earlier. He took her face in his hands, 'Tiff, look at me. You are not alone. I'm here for you and I'm not going anywhere.' He lent down and kissed her softly. This time, Tiffany returned his kiss, in an effort to fill the void of loneliness within her.

Kayla entered the kitchen. 'About time you two got it on. You've been like two lovesick teenagers for weeks.'

Tiffany jumped back from Harley. Warmth flooded her cheeks as she smiled to hide her embarrassment.

'Why are you in the kitchen? I thought you had more important things to attend to tonight,' Harley said gruffly.

'I heard about the baby and I just wanted to say sorry to you, Tiff. Obviously, you are devastated. You know what I think you need at a moment like this?'

Tiffany shrugged her shoulders. She was never sure what crazy suggestions Kayla might make.

Kayla walked towards Tiffany with arms outstretched. 'You need a Tiffany Sandwich.' Within a split-second, Tiffany found herself squashed between Harley and his sister in a three-way hug and in that moment, she came to the realisation that having a baby was not the only way to remedy her loneliness.

The End

THANK YOU

I hope you enjoyed 'Only the Lonely'. Thanks for taking a leap of faith to read an independent author's novel. It is hard to have cut through in such a saturated book market, so I would be thrilled if you could leave a review for this book on Amazon and Goodreads.

Thank you also to my trusted beta readers, in particular to Lisa Kenway, Aimee Quinlan, Tammi Watson and Sally Trethewy for their comments and support.

A big thank you to Daniel Kennard for his feedback on this book from a legal perspective, which helped me ensure the court scenes in this story are authentic.

There are a team of people who have helped me get my book to publication stage, so I would like to thank Laura Wilkinson for editing, Les at German Creative for the cover design and all the wonderful book bloggers who have taken time to give this novel a shout out.

I must also thank Alison Brown, from my local independent bookstore, for supporting me and selling my novels.

Last but not least, I would like to thank my family for their love and support. My husband Scott is my rock and even though he doesn't like reading fiction, he will always take the time to read my novels – now that is true love.

ABOUT THE AUTHOR

Joanne Nicholson is an Australian author who enjoys boating, exercising, reading, writing, music and spending quality time with family and friends.

Joanne's career began in advertising and marketing. After a hiatus to raise her four children, she owned an indoor play centre, worked in property management and bookkeeping. Joanne gave these up to focus on her passion for writing.

To follow Joanne you can find her at:

Facebook @joannenicholsonauthor

Twitter @jolnicholson

Instagram @joannenicholsonauthor

Or, visit her website:
www.joannenicholsonauthor.com

OTHER NOVELS BY JOANNE NICHOLSON

After spending her twenties travelling and living a carefree life, Ruth dreams of getting married and having a family. In her mid thirties and with her biological clock ticking loudly, Ruth goes to extreme lengths to become a mother. She is in shock when she finally gets a positive pregnancy test result back from the doctor, as well as being advised that she is now HIV positive.

With the love and support of her friends and family, she adapts to her new state of being and prepares for the challenges ahead of living with HIV and becoming a single mum.

Set in Australia, this contemporary fiction novel explores the modern day conundrum of internet dating, IVF and raising a child as a single parent.

A memory of Lily's late Mum prompts her to do a past life regression to see if they were linked in a previous life. Although skeptical at first, Lily soon finds herself travelling back through memories of her current life and then her previous life in the town of Bathurst, Australia in the early twentieth century. Lily is surprised to find out she was a male and her Dad in this life was her brother in her past life.

Wanting to confirm the facts of the regression were real, Lily researches the property she saw in her memories and discovers Elizabeth, her little sister from her past life, is still alive. Curiosity leads Lily to contact Elizabeth to see what she is like as an elderly woman and to test whether they have a connection in the present.

When Chloe finds out she has inherited a skill that will allow her to learn to read minds, she is excited to have an insight into what people think and feel. Initially, mind-reading appears to be an amazing gift as Chloe excels at work, using her skill to manipulate clients.

However, Chloe soon comes to the realisation that those people closest to her rarely say what they think. She is heartbroken to find out that her best friend lusts after her husband and that her husband fantasises about other women.

Unable to stop her mind-reading, Chloe is left with the dilemma of how she can live with her new found skill. Chloe's life takes on an unexpected new direction as she adapts to reading minds.

SHORT STORIES BY JOANNE NICHOLSON

A tropical holiday in Mexico seems the perfect way to celebrate a milestone birthday for four Australian women. Cocktails, sunshine and mariachi bands make this a trip of a lifetime, however their dream holiday turns into a nightmare when they are kidnapped and held for ransom. This short story touches on how each of the girls deals with this traumatic event differently.

When a little old gentleman goes into a bustling café to place an order for coffee he is ridiculed and humiliated for not being able to place his order electronically. Upset, he slams down a tattered old magazine on the counter, telling the crowd that karma will come back to haunt them.

As each person who picks up the discarded magazine reads their horoscope, they are surprised to find that it is accurate – but maybe not in the way they first imagined.

After reading this short story, you may not look at your horoscope in the same way ever again!

Author: Joanne Nicholson
Editor: Laura Wilkinson
Book cover design: GermanCreative